PRIMAL LUST

WILLOW WINTERS

PRIMAL LUST

PART I

Scarred Mate

CHAPTER ONE

MY PALMS AND KNEES ROUGHLY scrape back and forth against the grass, my nails digging into the dirt as my body pushes forward with every pleasure-filled thrust. Every nerve ending in my body is sensitized and even the moans that slip from my lips seem to add to my insatiable desire. My head hangs low, then rises with a desperate need to cry out as I take the punishing fuck. Devin's grip on the curves of my ass is so powerful that I wouldn't be surprised to find bruises later. His sharp fangs graze the tender skin on my neck, causing my blood to heat and rush through my veins with intense need. Arching my neck for him, I give him easy access to bite me, to claim me as his.

Every move is achingly natural and primitive; dark and seductive under the full moon.

"More," I say, whimpering my plea. His hips pound against mine as his pace quickens. Devin's thick girth stretches me fully, giving a hint of pain to the waves of pleasure crashing through me. It's instantly forgotten as overwhelming heat builds in my core. It spreads slowly through my body as my toes numb. *Yes, yes!*

As he slams into me, the force of his powerful thrusts pushes my body forward, nearly knocking me to the ground. Strangled moans escape me as he continues to pound into me without holding back, the beast in him taking over, fueled by the full moon. It's all so intense and my head thrashes as I fight the urge to pull away.

Too much. Too much.

I almost cry out for him to stop but I hold myself back, clenching my teeth and submitting to the overwhelming and all-consuming haze of passion, loving his fierce desire to claim my body with his.

Devin gently kisses my back, a move that's at odds with his forceful motions. Again his fangs glide across the skin of my neck, threatening to pierce me, to mark me and scar me forever as his. I groan in approval at the thought. I desperately want to be his. I *need* to be his. I moan my pleasure into the chill of the air, knowing I'm his to claim.

He owns me: my body, my heart, my future.

The unrelenting heat threatens to burn me as he pistons his hips harder and faster. I whisper the words "I can't," as he nips my ear, sending a fresh wave of pleasure to my throbbing core. Refusing to slow his pace, a low growl rumbles in his chest. I gasp for air as my body gives out and he slams into me to the hilt. His fangs finally give me what I've been wanting. They pierce into my sensitive skin, and I let out a scream at the agonizing sensation.

A sharp pain attacks my body, making every inch of me shake violently. Fire courses through my veins, blistering my skin and threatening to choke me. Just as I register the pain, a soothing wave of unmatched pleasure rocks through me, easing the burn and forcing me to tremble with sated desire.

"Mine." Devin licks the deep marks on my neck. Devin's hot tongue soothes the claiming bite. The intensity subsides as the cool wind caresses my exposed skin. "Mine."

"Yours. I'm yours." I say the words quickly as I try to catch my breath. His long, warm exhale against my skin causes goosebumps to flow down my shoulders as he licks his mark again and then nuzzles into the crook of my neck. His strong arms pull my feverish body into his muscular chest.

"I love you, Devin." My eyes refuse to open as I nestle into his embrace and sigh with contentment. I am his mate. Feeling overwhelmed with the emotion consuming my every thought, I leave kisses on his chest, his neck—every inch of him. I don't know how it's possible to feel this kind of love so quickly, so assuredly.

"I love you, Grace." Hearing the tender words spoken in his deep voice has my heart swelling in my chest. My limbs continue to tremble as he holds me tighter.

A small smile pulls at my lips until the heat in my veins slowly returns, demanding attention. I struggle not to pull away from my mate, my Alpha.

The sensation tightens my throat with a fire that's unsettling.

"It feels like I'm choking." I murmur the words, writhing in his grasp. He doesn't react except to pull me closer to him. As if he didn't hear at all.

I need air. I need this burning to stop. Every inch of my body feels superheated, growing hotter and hotter with every passing second. Fear latches on to me as I push away from Devin. The cold ground calls to me, promising me respite from the unrelenting heat. His arms tighten rather than loosen and I struggle against him. "I'm too hot." I can barely push out the words. The feeling of my breath against my face is too much. It's too hot. My hands shake, and my muscles tighten all at once. I try to push away again, but a dizziness overwhelms my body. Anxiousness washes over me. I'm not okay. Something's wrong. Something's very wrong.

"Shh, sweetheart. It'll be over in a minute. I've got you." His words are a soothing balm, and paired with his dominance, I'm able to settle for a moment. It's a much-needed reprieve. Devin rubs soothing circles on my back as he licks his mark. His touch calms me and his tongue soothes the burn. I manage to take one deep breath, and then another. The burning slowly wanes, starting at my neck and cooling in small waves down my body. The cold sweat that's left makes me feel even more tired. I lie limp in his arms, knowing I'm safe. Knowing he can comfort me and heal my pain.

It's only then my racing heart seems to steady and beat in tandem with his.

"Why?" I don't have the strength for more words, but I know he won't need any more. He'll tell me what I need to know.

"The essence of my wolf is claiming you. It will scent you as my mate." Devin gently pulls away from me to look into my eyes and I whimper from the loss of his calming touch. "Everyone will know you are mine. Only mine. Forever."

With his hand around my throat, he lowers his lips to mine and kisses them lightly. Before he says the word, I feel it, I hear it even, just a moment before. "Mine."

Exhausted, I lie in his arms, feeling the heat turn to warmth as my body slowly comes down from the high and adapts to the effects of his mark. My eyes close as he kisses my hair, murmuring words of love and devotion.

At the sound of a sob, my brow furrows and I pick up my head, immediately on alert. *Lizzie?* Brushing Devin aside, I whip around to my right to find her somewhere in the dark. "Lizzie?" I whisper as I try to creep from Devin's lap. His stubble gently scratches the shell of my ear as he shakes his head.

"It's not her, sweetheart." His voice carries a hint of anguish. Oddly, I feel it. That worry, that knowing concern, in a way, is present deep in the pit of my soul. I glance up at him and then follow his gaze to the gap in the tree line where we entered the clearing. Off to the left I make out the tall form of Veronica. She's alone and another sob rips through her as my eyes focus in the dark. She's hunched on the ground and crying. I scan the area for Vince, but he's nowhere to be found.

"He left her?" First disbelief, then anger runs through me, awakening my senses and energizing my limbs. How could he leave his mate crying? She must be in pain! The very thought she's suffering from his bite, from that unbearable heat, has me nearly in tears. *How could he leave her alone to suffer?*

"It's not what you think. She's not in pain. She's not human, so she won't be feeling the same as you. She may not even feel anything at all."

"How could she not feel anything? How could she not feel *that?*"

He chuckles and my instinct is to strike him for it. A member of our pack is broken down and alone. "She needs us." He must hear the insistency of my comment because his grip tightens and his voice lowers to a serious timbre.

"They're working through other things right now. It's best to leave them be."

My head shakes of its own accord. "She needs someone." My whispered plea begs him to understand. Regardless of whether or not she felt the pain of Vince's mark, she's obviously hurting from something. "I want to go to her." I've already started to stand as I make the statement, but Devin's powerful arms constrict around my body.

"It's best not to interfere." His words are hard and his tone is absolute.

How can he be so cold? A moment passes and she sobs again, crying out for Vince.

"I can't sit here and do nothing. She needs someone." His eyes soften at my words and his grip loosens. He doesn't say anything, merely gazing into my hazel eyes before nodding his head and releasing me.

As I step out of his hold and walk toward her, I'm suddenly very aware of the fact that I'm naked. Cold and naked, to be exact. With my arms crossed in front of me, I gather my courage and set the thought aside. They're shifters, they don't care.

Well, she's a vampire, but I doubt she'll mind.

Another soft cry for Vince is barely heard in the distance and any thought of modesty vanishes.

She needs me. I feel a pull to her. A pull to my pack as I get closer to her. It's a strange sensation that I haven't felt before, almost like a pressure in my chest is pushing me forward, urging me to comfort her. My hand rubs at the hard knot growing in my chest as the pain becomes impossible to ignore.

I approach slowly until I'm able to see her more clearly. Streams of blood leak down her face. Tears? She blinks and the whites of her eyes return to normal before clouding with the dark red liquid yet again.

The terrifying sight is both shocking and frightening, and I gasp while taking a hesitant step back. At my reaction, Veronica's head pulls up in a nearly violent fashion. My heart pounds and I can't control the natural instinct. When her eyes catch sight of me, she immediately rises, and in a blink, she's gone. Nothing but a blurred vision.

She vanishes so quickly, I don't believe it at first. I question my own senses. Did she run? *Holy shit.* How is that possible? I'd heard that vampires were fast, but to see it is something else entirely. Something eerie and startling.

I swallow a scream as Devin's hand comes down

on my shoulder. My beating heart slows once I realize it's him.

"She ran." I don't know what else to say.

"I saw. I thought she would. Like I said, it's best not to interfere. It's complicated, Grace."

My head shakes at his words. "No. She's not okay. She needs someone. I need to help her. I felt a pull to her."

His tone changes at my admission. "You felt a pull?" He turns me in his arms to look at me. "You felt a pull?" he repeats. I nod at his question. That's exactly what I felt. I rub my chest remembering the slight pain and growing knot. That's all but gone now. "I felt a physical need to go to her."

Devin lips turn up slightly into an asymmetric grin of pride.

"You were meant to be an Alpha, sweetheart. Fate has given me a strong mate."

"An Alpha?"

He nods his head. "An Alpha feels the needs of his pack. And sometimes those who aren't even his responsibility. You," he says as his hand cups my chin and lifts my lips to him for a sweet, soft kiss, "you are an Alpha." I smile against his lips, his words warming me with satisfaction.

Pulling back slightly, I manage to remember Veronica through the needy haze of my heat returning. "Where do you think she went?"

"I'm not sure. Vince is going to her now, though." My confusion at his knowledge dissipates as I remember their ability to communicate even at long distances.

"But how will he find her?"

"He'll always be able to find her. She'll never be able to run from him. Not now that he's claimed her."

I look back at the direction she ran. "But what if she doesn't want him to find her?"

He shrugs. "I suppose she'd have to keep running. Vampires are much faster than werewolves. She could outrun him forever, but she won't." I look back into his silver gaze questioningly. He gives me a small smile and a peck. "She may want to run now, but she needs him. And she knows it just as much as he does."

CHAPTER TWO

Grace

Y BODY IS SO DAMN SORE AS I WALK down the hall to Vince and Veronica's room. Every movement makes me ache, but there's also a deep sense of satisfaction knowing it's from being claimed by my Alpha. A simper slips across my lips as my fingertips graze the wound on my neck. The moment I touch it, as if to check that it's still there, I wish I hadn't. I wince from the gentle touch. *Fuck*, it hurts.

I remember being stunned this morning when I first looked in the mirror. My entire neck is bruised and his mark looks horrendous. It's going to take a week or more for it to heal. Devin spent most of the morning licking and kissing it. A familiar heat rolls through my body at the remembrance and the pain is so easily forgotten.

The sigh of contentment is met with regret as my gaze settles on Vince and Veronica's door. Taking a moment to shake out my hair, I wipe the grin off my face. This isn't what Veronica needs. I can already feel the venom she would give me if I were to prance in with puppy love, no pun intended, written across my expression.

An image of her disheveled and broken appearance last night flashes in my mind and my heart drops, although my pace doesn't slow. I have no business going to her with my happiness so damn evident. I clear my throat and compose myself before knocking hesitantly on the door.

Thump, thump, my heart is only given a single second before the doorknob turns.

Veronica opens the door slowly and raises her brows when she sees me. Given how well vampires hear, it's obvious she's not surprised to see me. Just surprised at the sight of my condition judging by how her gaze travels over my plain white V-neck tee and dark gray sweatpants. I was a bit too sore for jeans.

"Well, that beast didn't take it easy on you, did he?" She steps away from the door, holding it open and allowing me to walk through.

My eyes widen at the sight of her in a deep burgundy satin robe. I nearly gape at her appearance. She looks just the same as she did yesterday—not during the ceremony, but before. The way she always looks, which is stunning. Her tanned skin is completely unmarked with the only exception being a very faint silver scar along her shoulder. I have to squint to make it out. *Seriously?* I look like shit, like my mate mauled me, and she gets to go back to looking like a runway model? *Not fair.* Swallowing the petty thought, I enter the room and feel slightly uneasy as she shuts the door behind me.

It's only when I clear my throat to speak that I notice how sore it is. If I had to put money on it, I'd bet Veronica's throat isn't hurting either. As I part my lips, I note how casual she appears while she makes her way to the window. She doesn't seem to be in distress like she was last night. She's entirely composed. There are so many questions that beg to be asked. So many thoughts filled with compassion and empathy that stay lodged in the back of my throat. Nothing is as I thought it would be.

Devin was right when he said it's complicated, and that's in addition to the significance and difficulties Veronica being a vampire already brings.

Before I can speak, she gestures to a high-back chair in the corner of the room by a desk. "Sit."

A brow of mine cocks up of its own accord. I hesitate and narrow my eyes, not liking her tone or the use of the word "sit." Flashbacks of my first night with Devin run through my mind.

With a corner of her lips pulling up, she adds easily, "Please," while gracefully lowering herself into the desk chair. She crosses her long legs, which causes the slit of her robe to fall open slightly, exposing even more of her. I glance around the room before taking my seat.

"Where's Vince?" My posture mirrors hers, both of us resting our hands on the arms of our respective chairs. Suddenly, it feels claustrophobic in here even though it's just the two of us.

I'm alone in a room with a vampire … although Veronica's lips perk up again, no doubt at the sound of my racing heart, her dark eyes contradict her countenance. Her gaze holds a sense of mourning in them that I wish I could ease.

"I heard you were coming, so I asked him to get

us coffee." I don't miss how she relaxes her posture, appearing far less dominating.

"You must've heard Lizzie and I are practically caffeine addicts." I grin, but Veronica simply stares back without any trace of humor. "Thank you, though." I'm quick to add, "That's really sweet of you." At the word "sweet," her crimson lips curve upward and a small huff of a laugh leaves her.

"Yes, I can be very *sweet*." The way she speaks makes me uneasy. Any semblance of ease vanishes. She stares back at me as though I'm her prey. I shift uncomfortably. She doesn't seem to want my company, and I find myself regretting my decision to comfort her. She obviously doesn't need it. I start to get up, but then that knot in my chest forms again. My hand flies to the center of my chest and I press on it to try to ease the discomfort.

"Are you all right?" There's a trace of concern in Veronica's voice.

Nodding my head, I plant my ass firmly back down in the seat. "It's funny you should be asking me that, because I came here to ask you the same question." As the words leave my lips, the hard pain dissipates, granting me freedom to breathe normally. Rubbing the spot, I'm amazed at how quickly it left me. I make a mental note to talk to Devin about what the hell just happened.

It's similar to the pull from last night. Something has changed and it demands attention.

In the silence, my eyes find Veronica's dark gaze. Her lips are pressed in a hard line.

"I'm fine. I was mistaken about something last night."

"Mistaken?"

Her eyes narrow and I hold my ground as a flare of anger passes through me. She was more than shaken last night, so beat down, yet she refuses to acknowledge it. It's none of my business, except that she's my pack and this damn restlessness prods me to push. Just like I have to with Lizzie.

My eyes widen at the realization that Veronica's pulling the same shit Lizzie does. I narrow my eyes right back at her and repeat the single word incredulously, "Mistaken?" She seems to be shocked at how brazen I am, but I'm not going to back down. This pull inside of my chest demands action.

My voice is tighter than I'd like when I ask, "Why were you crying?"

Veronica clicks her tongue while searching my

eyes before she purses her lips. "Why does it matter to you?"

"I hurt for you. You're a member of my pack and I want to help you."

"I don't need help, little human." Her wicked grin returns and her hard mask resurfaces. "How could you possibly help me?"

"I can't answer that question until I know what the problem is." I stare straight back at Veronica, unaffected by her arrogant tone. She's not going to fool me any longer. We all have walls we build, brick by brick, to keep ourselves protected. Hers have tumbled down and I'll help her rebuild them if she needs, but only if that's the boundary she needs. My teeth sink into my bottom lip wondering if I should push her, and if so, how much harder.

Her shoulders relax and she leans back in her chair while tapping her bloodred nails on the desk. "I didn't like last night." Her cool expression and flat tone are at least a bit more genuine. I'll take the small opening she gave me.

"You didn't want him to claim you?"

She shakes her head gently. "It's not that. I'm honored to be his mate. I really am." She takes a deep breath and adds, "I didn't know fate would give me a mate at all."

"I don't understand. Don't you all have mates?"

Her response is to give me a soft smile that doesn't reach her dark brown eyes. "No, only werewolves, dear." She watches her fingers tap along the desk for a moment before continuing. "Other shifters too, I suppose." She breathes in heavily before meeting my questioning gaze. "Not vampires. We don't have mates."

"But you have Vince?"

"Only because Vince has me as a mate. Fate's a cruel bitch." She snorts a laugh although there's no humor in what she said.

"Why is it cruel?"

"Well, for starters, she gave Vince a bitch for a mate. And then for me …" Her voice trails off and she straightens in her seat before staring into my eyes. "Fate decided to give me a mate. One person to love for my entirety. I will love him with everything I have, but I will live much longer than he will. I will watch him grow old, while I am ageless. I will hold his hand when he dies, yet I will live." Red tears brim around her eyes as she smirks.

"Like I said, fate's a bitch. I never planned this."

She huffs that same humorless laugh. "I never wanted this. I never thought I'd have someone to love. And now that I have it, I'm not sure that I should. I wasn't made for this. It's not what I am." Her voice turns hard at the end and it makes my body stiffen with fear. She's a roller coaster of emotion ranging from disbelief to sadness and ending in anger. At first I'm taken aback by her honesty, but then I focus on what she said.

"You never thought you would love?" She can't truly mean that. "Do vampires not have the ability to love?"

She laughs, with real humor this time, and leans back in her seat while wiping away the blood rimming her eyes. I grimace inadvertently at the sight and unfortunately she sees my reaction.

"You don't know much about vampires, do you?"

"No. I'm sorry, I didn't—" She cuts me off before I can fully apologize.

"I've been a vampire for nearly two hundred years and I still despise some aspects of our species." She wipes her fingers on a tissue and places it on the desk as if she knows she'll need it again before trashing it; the bright red is vibrant against the stark white. "If I could change it, I would."

"You're two hundred years old?" Holy fuck. I don't have enough self-control to contain my shocked expression.

"Something like that." Her voice is flat. Then she tilts her head and a glint of happiness sparkles in her eyes. "Would you like to know how I came to be immortal? How I was changed?" Her smile widens, revealing her sharp white fangs. "I wasn't always like this." She shakes her head. "Vampires are a capricious species."

I clear my throat. From what I learned of vampires in school, that sounds about right. But then again, humans in general don't know much about them.

"Tell me." She quirks a brow and I suppress my smile. "Please." Her grin grows as we share a knowing look.

"I was a little older than twenty. I don't remember what day my birthday was because it's been so damn long. I was unmarried because I had been raised religious and thought I would become a nun. The day everything changed happened sometime around summer. I know that because there was a big thunderstorm that had just passed through our area, and where I lived the rainy season began in June." She rocks gently, glancing out the window as if watching her recollection playing out before her like she's watching a movie.

"I was in the rainforest foraging for my grandmother. She sent me out all the time to gather things. My mother and father had both passed away when I was a baby, leaving me alone with my grandmother to raise me by herself. She was in good health for her age and took care of me as any mother would." A sad smile pulls at her lips. "She always said I looked like my mother." That humorless huff of a laugh erupts from her throat. "I don't remember her at all. I used to be able to, but it was so long ago that I can't even picture her face anymore." Veronica falls silent as she tries and fails to recall her memory.

"I'm sorry." My voice brings her back to the present. Her dark eyes find mine and her grin returns.

"Don't be, dear. My first twenty years were good years. Even if I suffered loss, I was still grateful for my life." She visibly swallows. "At least until that day." I settle into my seat as I watch her pull her legs into her body. "I was gathering pandan leaves in the rainforest when I found some mangoes. They were delicious; I remember that well. They were nearly overripe but I'd cut one open to taste it. Fruit is best when it's almost too sweet, don't you think? It was a little treat for me. A reward for going out for my grandmother."

Her smile fades and her voice drops as she continues her tale. "I traveled to my usual area, where I knew I'd be able to find most of what she'd asked for. I was at the last pandan plant with only half of my basket full. I knew she'd need more leaves, so I went out a little farther. There was a large clearing and on the other side I spotted more bushes. The storm the previous night had left downed trees and broken branches in its wake, but somehow this clearing had been spared. It was so pretty. Undisturbed with dewdrops clinging to everything and sparkling in the light. So pure. I almost felt bad crossing through it to get to the other side." She gently shakes her head again and swallows. "But no one lived close to us and I didn't think I'd ruin it for anyone but myself. So I continued into the other side until my basket was full." Her lips pull down in a frown. "I knew my grandmother would be grateful. She would've been so happy to have a full basket."

Leaning forward in my seat, I clasp my hands. A hard pit forms in my stomach and my blood chills. I can tell I'm not going to like what I hear next. She clears her throat, but her dark eyes stay focused on her nails, tracing over the grain pattern in the walnut desk. She nods her head slowly. "I knew something bad was going to happen when I got back to the clearing. I could see so many large footprints in the dirt. They came from the left. I remember thinking there may have been four of them." The red tears brim in her eyes and spill over, trailing streaks of blood down her light brown skin. I part my lips, but before I can speak, she continues. "They were werewolves. I saw them shift in front of me. Well, two did. Two didn't." Her breath hitches.

"I don't have to tell you everything they did. But know that I didn't value my life afterward. I wished they'd just killed me. Instead, they left me mangled and damaged after they'd had their way with me. I was covered in bruises and bleeding out from the injuries they'd inflicted on me. Some of the plants I'd gathered had medicinal qualities; I used them to staunch my wounds. I still don't know how I made it back without dying. It was the longest journey of my life. Part of me wanted to stay and just succumb, but I was so scared they would come back."

"Where did you go?" I whisper the question, not sure I want to hear more but knowing I have to.

"Back to my grandmother's. Where else could I

have gone? It was two hundred years ago. There were no phones to call for help. We lived in such a remote area, there were no hospitals nearby. The shamans in our area had all left due to religious persecution. There was no one but her." Her sad smile returns and she laughs before she tells me, "She scolded me. When she heard the door open, she yelled from the kitchen that I'd scared her and to never do that again. And then she came out and saw me.

"She looked so broken when she saw me. When she saw my bruised body and she realized what happened. I was barely clothed and covered in blood. My grandmother was a truly devout Catholic. She said the church would help us, that they would know what to do." She reaches across the desk for the crumpled tissue and regains some of her composure before continuing. "It took forever to reach the local priest, but he accused me of making everything up. That I must have imagined what I saw and experienced because werewolves would never do such a thing." She straightens and faces me. "They were supposed to protect us. We had a pact with them. Apparently they were allowed to do whatever they wanted so long as the vampires were kept at bay. What happened to me was nothing more than a small sacrifice in exchange for the security they provided." Her dark eyes harden as she spits out, "That's what the priest told me. 'It was a small sacrifice to pay!' That's the day I started to hate everyone. My grandmother was the only one who wanted justice. No one else dared to confront the wolves." She calms herself and wipes her eyes again. I can't even fathom her pain. To live through something so monstrous and survive, only to experience a horrible betrayal—my heart breaks for her with the injustice of it all.

"She died a few weeks later. I think the church's refusal to intervene was too hard on her. She was so angry at everyone else and felt like she had failed me, even though there was nothing she could have done differently. Her heart just couldn't take it. So I was left on my own, on the outskirts of the town. I lived in fear that the shifters would come back. One night I thought they did. I thought they'd come for me again." A wicked glint shines in her brown eyes. "But it wasn't the wolves." Her dark red, plump lips form an evil smirk. The look on her face is one of a scorned woman who's reaped her revenge. "No, it was three vampires. They'd come to kill everyone." She tilts her head and I hear her neck crack as she reclines in her seat and crosses her legs. Her characteristic collected facade replaces the emotional woman who I'd just been sitting with.

"They were going to kill me. Most of the town had already been slaughtered. They decided to punish everyone who'd sided with the wolves. Not that we had much of a choice in the matter of what the werewolves did. Obviously. When they saw me, they smiled. Like we were old friends. They'd heard what the wolves had done and offered me a choice: death or the chance to have vengeance. If I'd been smart, I would have chosen death. But then again, fate wouldn't have been able to curse my poor pup had I died all those years ago."

"You'd rather have died than become a vampire?"

She shakes her head and purses her lips. "Not now, no. But the things I did, all out of hate and to get revenge ..." Her dark eyes narrow as she meets my stare. "There can be no forgiveness for all the innocent lives I've taken and all the times I sat back and watched as my coven ravaged villages for sport."

"Does your coven still ..." I swallow hard, not able to get out the rest of the words.

"My old coven, I'm not sure. If they do, then they must be keeping quiet about it. The Authority has no use for those who make messes they have to clean up."

"So your old coven is the one who trained you. Natalia?"

"Natalia's a bitch." Her voice is hard and dripping with spite. "She was there when I was made a vampire. She taught me some things, although she's not as good as she thinks she is. Hate motivated me for decades, but when the years pass like days, you learn to let some things go in the name of self-interest. Natalia's still fueled by malice. I've no idea why, but I tired of her antics long before I'd even left that coven."

"What about your current coven?" Part of me is intrigued, wanting to meet more vampires and hear their stories; the other part is terrified.

"They're … vampires. There's not much to say beyond that truth." She stands up and heads to the door, opening it just before Vince enters. "You took your time, didn't you?"

He only huffs a humorless laugh, each hand holding a coffee. Vince's silver eyes find mine and he smiles, although it's subdued. "Hey, Grace," he says. Veronica may seem the same as she did before last night, but something has shifted in Vince. Something darker, something more careful.

Veronica asks Vince to give me my drink and holds the door open, telling me, "You can go now."

"I was really hoping to talk to you a bit more." Glancing between the two of them, I'm left feeling like an intruder.

"I'm happy you came to see me, sweet mate of my Alpha, but Vince will take care of me." Vince looks up from setting her coffee on the dresser and gives Veronica a semblance of a smile.

"I've got her, Grace." I feel the need to pry and protect Veronica, even if she doesn't think she needs it, but something in me settles and I know that I can leave them be. Something deep inside me is telling me that Vince will heal her. He is her mate. As I head back to the east wing of the estate, I expect the knot to form in my chest, objecting to my leaving. I rub my chest as I walk back to my room, waiting for the pull, but it never comes.

CHAPTER THREE

"**W**HAT DOES YOUR COVEN WANT with the blood bank?" My hardened and blunt tone doesn't seem to bother Veronica. Good. I'm glad she's taken to her position in the pack easily enough. Unlike my mate, who's still finding her feet and second-guessing herself. She's doing well, though.

It's not until Veronica answers that I realize my thoughts have drifted to Grace yet again. Even with treachery at hand and the threat of war, all I do is think about Grace. *I'm an obsessed wolf.*

"There isn't nearly enough blood to sustain our

coven. We don't venture into human territory much and we don't reside near wildlife." Her nose scrunches in distaste. "More than that, purchasing blood from the Authority costs far too much for far too little." Her sharp nails tap on the counter once before she adds, "It seemed wiser to go directly to the banks."

"You have to order the blood for the coven?" It's difficult to keep my expression impassive. Much about vampires remains a mystery, even to other supernatural species. So long as laws aren't broken, they aren't required to divulge any information regarding any aspects of their way of life. There are plenty of whispers, though …

"We don't *have* to order blood. But most of the humans won't sell theirs and like I said, our sources for acquiring it are limited."

"What about having a personal …" I leave the remaining words unspoken.

"Drinking from humans? From their necks? It's been outlawed, as I'm sure you know."

"And your coven abides by the law?"

She swallows thickly, her gaze dropping for a fraction of a second before she nods.

"I see." When I see him, I'll be sure to ask Alec about the blood they sell to the covens. If they're drugging blood from the humans' blood banks, then I'm certain they'd be tainting the blood they sell to the covens as well. A tic in my jaw spasms. Thank fuck we don't drink that shit, but Veronica might.

"And do you plan on drinking the blood from the banks?" I don't miss that her body stills and tenses. "I *need* to know." Not only for her protection; I need to be sure she isn't a part of this scheme to poison other immortals. I'm fairly certain she has nothing to with it, but the way she glances at Vince and instinctively touches her neck where his claiming bite is, has my stomach knotting. As if she thinks being his mate will protect her if she's a part of anything as fucked as tainting blood.

Drawing herself to her full height, Veronica responds loud enough for Vince to hear, "If you'd rather I didn't drink from him—"

"Fuck that! What the fuck, Devin?" Vince's aggression takes me by surprise but as always, my face stays expressionless. My eyes narrow as they meet his and he backs down, no doubt feeling my anger.

"I want her to drink from me." His hands fist at his sides, but he relaxes them, reining in the initial indignation.

"He's your Alpha." Veronica's hushed words seem

to relax him a bit. As Vince comes closer, sidling up to the counter in the kitchen, Veronica's hand gentles on his arm. The touch is light but meaningful.

"This has nothing to do with her drinking from you." A look of relief flashes across Veronica's face. It appears she was only worried I'd make her stop drinking from Vince. Instantly her posture relaxes.

"Good. I want her to," Vince answers and then slides out a stool, the legs of it scraping against the floor as he does.

"So, you two are breaking the law?" I allow a little lightheartedness to enter my voice so Vince will calm the hell down.

Vince nods, letting a smirk grace his lips as he nods at me. "I'm a rulebreaker, Alpha," he jokes, but Veronica is less flippant.

"My entire coven is breaking the law. Most are pissed about the decree, but Natalia is essentially an inquisitor. She regularly visits our queen and the heads of the other covens. I was sent to observe members of the Authority after the queen's son was taken and punished for disobeying Natalia."

"He drank from a human?"

She nods. Vince's attention is focused on Veronica now, the reality sinking in hard that the Authority may step in. His anxiety and anger mix into a cocktail that's practically fucking palpable.

"Where did they take him?"

"To the Authority. To their dungeon. He was given a thousand lashes."

"A thousand?" The surprise is evident in Vince's voice. "A thousand silver lashes?"

She nods once and adds, "He was nearly dead when Natalia brought him back."

"For drinking from a vein?" How the hell is that reasonable?

"He did it in front of Natalia. The bitch had two enforcers take him in the middle of the night. Had they been seen, it would have been war. When she returned him, my queen nearly sent the entire coven to exact vengeance on the Authority. But she put her emotions in check, realizing it wouldn't have been wise. Not when we're so greatly outnumbered."

Vince's pulse still races. Not from fear of lashes, but from the danger his mate is in by staying at a coven clearly on the Authority's radar. His thoughts race but I silence them with a wave of my dominance as his Alpha.

"They allowed this?" I can't fathom that Alec would allow such violence. A thousand lashes just for drinking from a vein. Before she can reply, I ask, "The person offering the vein, they were willing?"

"She was willing. She's his partner. What's even more offensive is that Natalia violates the law herself. She only drinks from a vein, I know she does." I consider her words as she shakes her head.

"How do you know?"

"I've seen her do it for over a century now." Vince wraps his arm around Veronica's waist and pulls her closer to him. She leans into his touch, her hip nestled against him. A smile threatens at the sight of the two of them on agreeable terms after last night, but I hold back.

I don't know what happened between them, but she didn't run like I thought she might.

Perhaps she feels more for him than she lets on. Or perhaps her coven is truly in need.

Desperate times and desperate measures …

"So that's why your queen sent you. Because her hand is being forced by the coven?" She nods once at my question. "And is it solely Natalia that's pushing the issue?"

"Mostly, but she has the backing of the other members. When they came to collect and imprison Stephan, she brought nearly a dozen other vampires with her."

"Was Alec there?" I hesitate to ask, but I have to make sure before I go to meet with him.

"No, only the vampires of the Authority." If I remember correctly, there are fourteen who are members of the Authority. That's more than most covens.

"Thank you, Veronica. Vince."

He immediately responds, "Yes, Alpha?" That's a much better tone, although he's tense. His emotions are unsteady and I consider him for a moment before speaking. I decide to let his anger from earlier go unchecked. After all, I've heard having a vampire drink from you can be quite an experience. She's his mate and he's made his boundaries clear. I'll respect that.

"Are you sparring today?"

He nods and elaborates, "Dom and Caleb are going to go at it. I have to be around to see that." He glances at his mate and smiles. "And I thought it would be fun for them to see what Veronica can do."

I nod in agreement. Natalia taught Veronica, so I have no doubt she can handle herself just fine.

"I'll have to watch her at some point as well." First I'll speak with Alec. Too much right now is uncertain. Alec will tell me what I need to know, and then I'll be able to take action. I'm responsible for the pack and my mate needs safety above all else.

CHAPTER FOUR

Dom

IZZIE LOOKS SO FUCKING SMALL ON THE sparring platform. My mate, my gorgeous mate. Last night was a damn dream come true. Holding her in my arms while I rutted into her tight pussy. I've waited all my life for her. She's mine now and she's eager to have me. A low, rumbling growl barrels through my chest at the memory of her soft whimpers and loud moans of pleasure. An asymmetric grin pulls at Caleb's chest when he hears the animalistic sound rip through me. She took us both just as she was made to.

"*Fucking perfect.*" He mutters in my head so only I can hear him. "*You think this is going to work?*"

I shrug my shoulders.

"*I have no idea, but it's worth a shot.*" We decided last night that teaching Lizzie to spar may help bring her wolf out again. She's only felt her the one time since the offering and although I'm happy her wolf returned, it's fucking tearing up my sweet little mate.

She's been traumatized and her wolf abandoning her is a reminder of that. No matter how much she smiles and pretends it doesn't get to her, she wants her wolf to come back and stay. She wants to shift so badly; I know she does. I have no idea if she'll ever be able to, but I'll do everything I can to help her.

"*Well, even if it doesn't coax her wolf out to play, she'll at least learn how to fight,*" Caleb comments and his thoughts turn darker. It's a side of Caleb I'm not comfortable with even if Lizzie is.

"You better not fucking bruise her." My statement, whispered aloud, carries a thinly veiled threat.

Caleb's reaction is dismissive. "*Have you seen our mate? I'm not the only one who's fucked up in our pairing, and if it's what she craves—*"

"*We should've taken it easier on her.*"

"*You didn't exactly think that last night,*" he rebuts.

The low growl is repressed as I tear my gaze from his. Shuffling my feet and kicking the floor, I avoid the sight of Lizzie's neck as guilt washes over me. Her hips are covered in bruises from where we gripped her, and her neck is covered in bites and bruises. Both of our marks are an angry red color.

I confess to him, *"I wish her wolf would come heal her. I hate seeing her so fucking wounded."*

"It might happen. It might not … but she fucking loved it."

His comment doesn't help loosen the growing knot in my chest. He continues, *"Did you see her looking at herself this morning? She was delighted to see our marks."* His shoulder bumps into mine as he speaks. *"She'll heal up nice and the only thing that'll be left are two silver claiming marks on her neck. Proof she's ours."*

Imagining her beautiful slender neck with our scars on her makes my chest puff out in pride with a warmth spreading through me.

"Damn right she's ours." At my inner words, Lizzie glances over to us and smiles while walking toward the edge of the platform. Her leggings are practically painted on and her sports bra leaves nothing to the imagination. I'm hard again just looking at her.

"So which one of you two is going to fight me?"

Her tone is flirtatious and a blush creeps up her chest to her cheeks as her gaze slips from mine to Caleb's.

"Both of us." Caleb's answer doesn't lack an ounce of sex appeal and she bites into her bottom lip, rocking slightly on her feet.

The flirtation is … well, it works her up. But he's out of his damn mind.

"She can't handle both of us," I tell him.

He chuckles at my words as he climbs into the ring and it takes me a moment to register why. When I do, I let out a huff of a laugh.

"She won't be able to fight either of us off right now, but she'll learn." He answers me loud enough for her to hear.

"All right." I concede and follow Caleb onto the platform just as I see Veronica and Vince heading our way. A prick of unease flows through me. Vince has been … off. He's bothered, and we can all feel it.

"Showtime isn't until later. We're training our baby girl first," Caleb calls out to them.

With the arrival of guests, Lizzie seems to second-guess our plans.

"Can I just watch?" Her tone makes it obvious she's a bit hesitant to get physical.

"Nope. You gotta learn a little something first."

Caleb's answer is immediate and casual, but as I remind him, she's been through a lot. Anything could trigger a trauma response. I want to avoid that if possible.

"I'm scared," she barely whispers as Veronica and Vince come up to the platform.

"Nothing to be scared of, baby." He kisses her left cheek. It's only a peck, but it soothes her instantly. The bond between mates will do that and the anxiousness I feel also dissipates.

"Fine." She draws her shoulders back and raises her little fists while backing up to the edge of the platform. "But I want a kiss for every punch I get in."

I chuckle at the sight of her. Our sweet mate has a lot to learn.

"First of all, don't back yourself into a corner. Never," I say.

Caleb nods his head in agreement with me and adds, "It's even worse when you're outnumbered. Now get your ass back here."

She immediately walks back to join us at the center of the ring. He moves her easily, so that she's facing away from us. "So I should just stand here and wait?" she asks.

Caleb eyes her ass as he answers and then slips his

hands around her hips before kissing her neck once again. "If you can't run, yes. Wait for your opponent to attack and watch carefully so you can block. Take your attacker off guard. If you can get in the first hit, make sure you make contact and really hurt them. Make it worth the energy."

"So if I can't run, hit first—" She's paying attention, even if Caleb appears to be preoccupied with other thoughts.

"Only hit if you can get a good hit in. If not, then you wait so you can block." Caleb interrupts her and I nod at his words although she can't see.

"How will I know if it'll be a good hit?"

"If you have easy access to the eyes, nose, throat or groin, then take the shot."

"Turn around and watch," I command her and she obeys instantly.

I put my hand up to Caleb's nose with my palm out and motion upward. "Like this, little one. That'll break the nose and push the bone into the brain."

Caleb turns sideways and elbows me in the gut. "Or shove your elbow right here. Clasp your hands and push with all your weight." The move knocks the wind out of me, but I only smile. "Cheap shot," I grunt.

"You want to try to land a hit instead of waiting for us to come from behind?"

She nods and says, "Yeah, let me try." Our little mate licks her lower lip, excitement running through her. It's a good sign.

"Any hint this has turned into anything … alarming … and I'm calling it off," I remind Caleb internally.

"Agreed," he answers back.

"All right," I offer to Lizzie, "I'm going to block it, but don't stop." She takes a deep breath and tries to palm strike my nose, but she's too damn slow and I'm able to snatch her wrist without much effort at all. "Faster, little one. Make it count."

She purses her lips when I release her hand, her eyes narrowing at the challenge. "But you know it's coming."

I nod my head at her deflated tone.

Caleb's arms are crossed over his chest as he tells her, "Your attackers may expect you to attack also. You have to be quick."

Appearing dejected, she rocks back and forth with her eyes on the ground. I part my lips and take a small step forward ready to comfort her, and that little hand of hers comes up from fucking nowhere and she actually lands the blow.

Square against my nose.

"Fuck!" My hands fly to my face. The stinging pain makes me wince and I think I'm bleeding.

Caleb's laughing his ass off and Vince is doing the same. I glance over to see Veronica full-on grinning, Vince's arm wrapped around her waist.

"Your girl got a hit on you, Dom. You a big softy now that you're mated?"

"Come on up here, Vince, and find out." That wipes the smile off his face; only for a second, though.

"Are you okay?" my mate questions softly. I don't miss the fact she's having second thoughts about this plan to coax out her wolf and her wide blue eyes are shining with vulnerability.

"Of course," I tell her and lean forward, giving her a peck on the right cheek, a twin kiss to match the one Caleb gave her earlier. Grinning down at her I add, "Now I know both you and Caleb take cheap shots."

That makes her genuinely smile and seeing her beautiful face light up fills my chest with warmth. The moment's interrupted, though … by her other mate.

"Good job, baby girl." Caleb gives her another small kiss on her cheek before raising his arms and getting into a boxing stance. "Now come get me, baby."

He looks ridiculous.

Lizzie just stands there shyly looking between the two of us. "You sure it's okay, Dom?" she says.

I chuckle at her concern and wipe my nose. The pain's already gone and I can feel it's mostly healed. "Yeah, little one. You did good. Now give me a kiss and don't ask again." She walks easily to me and brushes those soft, sweet lips of hers against mine. A rumble of satisfaction settles in my chest. I take a step back. "I wasn't expecting that one. You did well to take advantage of the situation and catch me off guard."

"Now we're ready, baby. Come on. It's not going to be easy." Caleb motions her forward and she practically lunges at him, aiming for his nose again. Caleb's quick to wrap his arms around her shoulders in a bear hug and tries to pull her into his chest to capture her, she quickly spins around so her back is to him. Shifting her hips, she drives an elbow into his side putting all her weight behind it. She moves fast. Faster than a human.

Caleb grunts and drops to the floor while I let out a bark of a laugh. I feel myself smile. Her eyes catch mine as I laugh and she stands confidently over Caleb's balled-up form.

Fuck, why does that turn me on like it does?

"You have such a beautiful smile," she tells me. Her kind words stoke the fire in me. I want nothing more than to pull her onto the ground and devour her body.

"*Not now, jackass.*" Caleb's words resonate inside my head and snap me out of it. I walk forward to reward my little mate with a kiss.

"You're a natural," I say. She leans into my touch and then looks to Caleb for a kiss from him. The small act makes me chuckle.

"Okay, how do I hit the groin? You didn't show me."

Oh, fuck that.

"Vince, get up here," I yell out to the now pale fucker who only stops laughing once I call his name.

"Nah, I'm good, man." I look at Caleb and open my mouth, but he beats me to the punch.

"I got the last hit. You can take this one." He walks to our little mate and kisses her cheek. "Hit him hard, baby. If you can get a knee to his groin, you'll get him on the ground for sure."

Lizzie's hesitant to ask something but before I can tell her to say whatever's on her mind she asks, "Are you two letting me get these hits in?"

I shake my head adamantly, as does Caleb. "Not

at all. I wasn't ready for that. You're much faster than I expected." His fingers brush the hair back away from her face while he leans forward and whispers to her, "You're as fast as a wolf. I didn't expect that." A blush creeps up her chest and into her cheeks.

"My turn," Veronica calls out from below. "You three obviously need a break before you start giving the two of us a different kind of show. Come, pup, I want to see what kind of damage you can do."

I take Lizzie's small hand in mine. "It will be good for you to watch." My eyes find Vince's. "And I'll enjoy watching Vince's mate beat the shit out of him." Caleb laughs on the other side of Lizzie before he pulls her hand to his mouth for another kiss.

She loves it when we kiss her. It keeps her smiling, keeps her happy. I imagine it keeps her thoughts from going elsewhere.

"Can we do it again after them?" Lizzie asks as we climb down.

"Of course. Especially now that we know you have some natural ability. Let's just take a moment, all right?"

I'm happy she took that as well as she did. I speak to Caleb in my head.

"Yeah, that's our mate, though. She's such a wild spitfire."

"Sometimes, but other times she's so shy."

"Well, she did just meet us, Dom. She's gotta have some time to open up." He has a good point. *"And I think she's doing wonderfully."* I nod at his silent words.

He drops her hand to wrap his arm around her waist, pulling her into him and slightly away from me. Her hand squeezes mine and it gives me enough satisfaction to not be jealous of his possessive move.

"You did great, baby. Next time we'll be ready for you, though." She blushes as he whispers into her ear. Settling down on the ground next to Lizzie, I look up to see Veronica and Vince circling each other. "This should be a good show." I pull Lizzie closer to me and Caleb grins as he sits on her other side, knowing exactly what I'm doing. He can deal with me pulling cheap shots too.

He leans back resting on his forearms and concentrates on the two sparring. "Vampires are faster than us. Much faster, but we have far more strength than they do," I say. Lizzie nods, acknowledging my words.

I watch her pale blue eyes widen as Veronica lands a blow to Vince's chest before dropping to the ground to avoid Vince's attempt to grab her. She slides easily between his wide-legged stance and stands behind him, landing a kick to his back before he's even registered what's happened. He lands on all fours but quickly recovers, leaping and spinning in midair to snatch her wrist as she strikes. She's completely unaffected by his hold and lands a punch to his throat, right on his Adam's apple. The blow makes him loosen his grip on her enough for her to jump back to the other side of the ring as his hands fly to his throat. Vince growls his frustration and the two circle each other again.

The first round goes to Veronica. By a long shot.

"Holy shit, it's like a blur," Lizzie breathes out the words, clearly in awe.

"Yeah," I answer, equally impressed although I expected this. Still, it's something else to watch a vampire move and fight. The unease from earlier returns.

"Do you see how she kept fighting without hesitation? He had a grip on her, but she didn't let that stop her attack." I speak quietly into Lizzie's ear while she continues to watch. "You need to have that same tenacity. Never stop fighting." I notice movement from the corner of my eye and I glance at Caleb as he nods his head and smiles.

"Never stop fighting, baby."

She smiles at his words, but immediately winces as Veronica kicks Vince hard in the chest. The telltale crunch of broken ribs resonates in the air.

Vince is knocked off-balance from the hit. Dropping to one knee, he's able to grab her ankle. She brings her other leg back and nearly lands another vicious kick to his face, but Vince tackles her to the platform with her beneath him. His crushing weight pins her in place. He releases her leg and reaches for her waist as she wriggles under him in an effort to get free. They wrestle for a moment and he pulls her hips toward his with a strong grip. Just as he smiles, thinking he's won, she throws her elbow back and it lands hard on his nose.

"Oh fuck," Caleb comments, his hand moving to his nose in empathy.

She's ruthless, and her skills are designed to take advantage of the natural instinct to protect the sensitive areas she targets.

"Oh!" Lizzie's hands flies to her nose too as she grimaces. Yeah, I know that fucking hurt. Vince doesn't release Veronica, though, which is obviously what she was counting on. Instead he drops all his weight onto her and his head lays against her back, caging her in. She struggles beneath him for a moment before realizing he's got her pinned. Despite her formidable fighting ability, she's physically outclassed in such a vulnerable position by his massive strength.

I barely hear Vince say "Gotcha" in a playful tone and then he kisses the crook of her neck. Veronica continues to struggle, though. Her breathing picks up until it's nearly panicked. Looking at Caleb, both confusion and concern are apparent on his face. Lizzie's shoulders hunch and she stirs uncomfortably between us.

"Get off of me!" Veronica shouts and pushes forcefully against Vince's massive frame. He props himself up on his knees, lifting his chest off of her back. In a blur of motion almost too quick to follow, she moves to stand on the other side of the ring.

Vince holds both his hands up while he stays still on his knees. "It's just me." Her shoulders rise and fall as her breathing slowly evens out. Slowly, he gets off the ground and walks calmly to her as if she's a cornered animal.

She swallows and shakes out her hair. "I know. I know." He takes her hand and leads her to the stairs.

"*What the hell was that about?*" I ask Vince in my head.

"Don't worry about it. I'll take care of her." I nod my head slightly as they walk past us. Lizzie looks to Veronica with concern in her eyes, but the vampire stares straight ahead, obviously still shaken and embarrassed by her reaction.

"She'll be all right, little one." I kiss her soft lips as Caleb rises.

"Come on, baby girl. We're going to show you how to block like Vince should've done." I snort at his words and help our little mate up, who's still watching Veronica leave.

CHAPTER FIVE

Veronica scowls when she sees the bed, her spine stiffening and she says, "You think you can chain me, pup?" There's humor in her voice and a little smirk on those beautiful full lips.

I love that nickname she's given me. *Pup.* The way the word spills from her lips makes my own lift in an asymmetric grin.

With every heavy step I take toward the pair of handcuffs dangling from the headboard, she follows behind me. I push aside the black velvet covering the cuffs so she can see the metal underneath. "They're

silver. You won't be able to break out of these, babe."
A thump in my chest makes me second-guess what
I'm doing as she gasps and then goes still. It's hard to
swallow with the flash of betrayal that lights across
her eyes. Only for a moment, though. She needs this.
She needs me to be a worthy mate. One who will heal
her as much as she's already healed me.

With her gaze focused on the bright metal, she
noticeably swallows. Her dark eyes find mine while
she shakes her head slightly.

My tone is soothing and I add a hint of play-
fulness although that thump in my chest happens
again. "Don't you trust me, baby?"

She hesitates, merely staring at the cuffs in my
hand. Eventually she settles on a muttered truth
spoken just beneath her breath. "I don't want to do
this."

I know she doesn't, but after seeing her trig-
gered and scared again today, I'm not going to wait
to show my mate she can trust me.

"How about if I promise to give you the key
and do everything you command me to do?" I offer
her. Her lips purse and she narrows her eyes. I need
to sweeten the deal. "It's just me, baby. Just me and
only for an hour." Her posture shifts slightly, but

she keeps her arms crossed tight over her chest. "Just one hour," I say softly, taking a step closer to her. My hand rests on her shoulder, but only for a moment before she leaves me.

Her dark eyes find mine again before she clicks her tongue and walks over to trail her fingers along the velvet covering the silver cuffs.

"I tied it up here too, in case you want to grip it. There's no way it'll touch your skin, baby." Her fingers slip inside the cuff. They're quality, the best I could find, and nicely padded. They won't hurt her at all.

"Why?" she questions.

"You're afraid of giving up control ... even when it comes to your mate."

Swallowing thickly, she stares back at me, the truth of my words sinking deep into her.

"I only exist for you. I would die for you. And you don't trust me." It fucking kills me to say it out loud. "I have to do something, Veronica."

"Fine," she states with an elegance and finality only a woman like her can deliver. "Do it quickly before I change my mind."

I smirk at her response, even as I see her shoulders rise and fall with her deep intake of breath, the deep red silk shining in the dim light as she does. She doesn't wait for me to undress her as she sits at the foot of the bed and lies back with her wrists lifted above her head. The thin straps of her nightgown slide down her shoulders and she doesn't bother to pull them back into place.

She'll have plenty of slack until I get to her legs.

Any bit of heated excitement turns bitterly cold as I watch her hold her breath and close her eyes when the cuffs snap in place around her dainty wrists. With a heaviness I never imagined I'd feel when it came to my mate, I tug the handcuffs to ensure they're snug and secure before moving to the cuffs at the foot of the bed.

The room is quiet. So quiet, the click of the last shackle locking around her ankle sounds impossibly loud. A shudder runs through her body as I take her in.

A gorgeous vampire, laid out on my bed clad in only a thin whisper of silk that hides next to nothing from me. My hand gentles on her calf as I prepare to test her restraints, but she beats me to it, yanking against the restraints.

"Key." She says the single word with authority although a hint of panic lingers.

I give her a tight smile and prepare myself for her wrath with gritted teeth as I slip the key in between her lips. Instantly her eyes widen as she spits the key out. "Give me the key!" Heated anger I've never felt from her before radiates off her. So much so, my wolf retreats.

She yells again, the pain and desperation she's feeling coming through clearly as I pick the key up off the floor and move closer to place it back in her mouth.

Her gorgeous frame struggles against the chains, but her arms don't move far enough to reach me. Even if she had the key in her hands, she'd be unable to unlock the cuffs. She's utterly at my mercy and I can see the moment she realizes she needs me to free herself. Sadness and betrayal flash across her face; in that instant I nearly regret my decision.

"You fucking dog!"

"It's just for one hour." My voice is soft, but stern. She needs this. She hisses at my simple statement. "I'm still yours, Veronica. I'll do whatever you say."

"Untie me!"

"Anything but that." Her nostrils flare and her

face reddens with rage. Her wrists pull against the restraints to no avail.

"If you come near me to do anything else … anything but untie me …," she trails off as I take a deep breath and lean close to kiss her cheek. Close enough for her to strike me with her fist across my jaw, which she does. I pull back, but I'm not far enough away to miss the second swing. The sharp, metallic tang of blood coats my mouth.

Fuck, my mate knows how to fight and make every blow count. The burning heat from her punches jolts me backward. I nearly fall off the bed, but I steady myself. "Babe, that hurt." I pinch my nose to stop the bleeding and straighten it before it heals crooked. Drops of blood fall to the comforter. As I feel my nose mending, I hear her sobs.

"Vince." She whimpers my name in between gasps. "Vince, I'm so sorry. Vincent."

Still hunched over, I wait until the pain of the blows has passed, until physically it no longer exists. It's only a memory.

I wipe my nose with the back of my hand and lean forward to kiss her on her tearstained cheek.

"Please forgive me. Forgive me, Vince, please. I'm so sorry. I—"

I cut her off, pressing her plump lips to mine and caress her face. "It's all right, baby. I knew you wouldn't like this. I knew …"

She shakes her head with her eyes shut tight and her lips pressed together, muting her panicked cries.

"It's not okay. It's not okay." Her words are rushed, a new panic taking over. "Vince, I'm sorry. I'm so sorry. I'm not okay."

I stroke her cheek until she opens her eyes and finds my silver gaze. "I forgive you, baby."

"I'm scared." She whispers the words before another tortured sobs erupts from her throat and she pulls against the chains again.

"It's all right, my love. I'm going to take care of you. I'm going to prove to you that you can trust me." Leaning in close, I kiss her again. Her mouth parts to grant me entry and I suckle her top lip before running my tongue along her sharp fangs.

"Please, Vince, I can't." She shakes her head and her deep brown eyes, rimmed in red, plead with me.

"I'm sorry, I can't. Not yet." Her head drops in defeat as she slowly nods and the sobs subside. "Give me a command, Veronica. I'm still yours."

Her dark eyes filled with red tears find mine and she says, "Hold me."

I lie down and settle my chest into her side before wrapping my powerful arms around her curves. I've never imagined her as this delicate before. I could easily crush her. She struggles against the shackles as another crying jag passes through her body; she trembles under my touch. A small part of me urges me to cave, not liking her reaction. My grip on her tightens. She needs this. She needs to learn to trust me. In time, I know she will.

"What do you want from me, Mistress?" I use her pet name, hoping that will calm her.

"I'm cold." Her softly uttered words contain a plea, not a command. Swallowing the lump in my throat, I pull the covers over our bodies and kiss the small dip in her throat.

"What else?" I need her to command me. I need her to find her strength.

"Just hold me." She sobs again and pulls against her chains as I lie back and gently place her head on my chest.

She cries silently. "I got you, babe. I promise." I barely speak the words, but my vow resonates through her, calming her. It hits me hard that she's not herself. She's not the strong, confident woman I know. She's so damn wounded. "I got you." I kiss her shiny black hair and let her cry.

Next time will be better. Next time I'll push her a little more. Until there is nothing between us but trust. Until she doesn't fear a damn thing in this world. Until she knows I will love her in her worst moments and through it all.

PART II

Blinded Obsession

CHAPTER SIX

Devin

EVERY WALL OF ALEC'S OFFICE IS LINED WITH shelves that run from floor to ceiling. They hold a priceless collection of ancient books that no doubt contain information lost to civilization over time. The dark wood of antique furniture polished to a high shine, yet bearing the marks of history, adorns the office. In the very center of the three-story room sits a heavy desk with books stacked high upon its glossy surface. Two leather wingback chairs have been placed across from it. The pendant lamp above Alec's desk encompasses an open flame.

matching the torches placed in sconces around the room.

If I wasn't aware that magic protects this space, I'd worry the texts would be in danger of being lost forever in a fire. It is common knowledge, though, that this room is heavily guarded by powerful wards.

I take a seat across from him and the old leather groans in protest. We're nearly matched in our attire: dark slacks and simple button-down shirts. Although my clothes are custom tailored to fit my body perfectly. A pair of wire-rimmed glasses peek out from his shirt pocket and today he's opted for a navy blue tie.

It's not the first time I've come to visit him here, but this is the first time it's been to deliver bad news.

"I'd almost forgotten how comfortable these chairs are," I say as I sit back. Alec's emotions are easily read. He allows his aura to coat the air around him. He's peaceful and the comfort of his office makes it simple to follow his lead and adopt a relaxed nature. Vaguely I wonder if he already knows why I'm here.

With a grin that emphasizes the wrinkles around his eyes, he nods agreeably. "I prefer for my guests to feel at ease. Although, you don't seem as comfortable as I'd like."

"It would help if I was here for a different reason." His small smile slips a bit and the air turns cold, but only for a moment. He parts his lips, but a quiet knock at the door stops him from speaking.

A petite blond woman with an upturned nose pushes through the door using her backside as she carefully handles a silver tray loaded with teacups and a teapot. She turns and gracefully strides to the desk.

She sets the tray down gently, jostling the cups only the faintest bit. With a deep breath, she offers Alec a bright smile. Her dark brown eyes seek Alec's approval, shining with obvious affection. A humorous smirk plays at his lips and his light blue eyes find hers.

There's unmistakable romantic tension between them. So much so that I'm given the impression I'm intruding and I readjust in my seat.

"Thank you, dear."

Dear. My brow lifts, although I attempt to hide my reason.

Her gorgeous smile widens further as she leans across the desk to give him a peck on the cheek. I hurriedly avert my eyes as her blouse slips, revealing a bit more than I think she realized. All the sight of the two of them does, is remind me of my own mate. I already long for her.

It's not until I hear the click of the door closing that I'm brought back to the present.

Back to Alec and the matters at hand.

"She seems very nice." Alec grunts a response and lifts the teapot.

"Just sugar? Is my memory correct?" I nod and eye the old sorcerer in front of me. With a heavy sigh, he finally acknowledges the obvious. "She's quite nice. I enjoy her company."

"I think she enjoys yours as well." His eyes dart to the door with longing before he clears his throat and passes me a teacup with its accompanying saucer.

The porcelain clinks and it doesn't escape me that the dainty dishes look completely out of place in my callused hands.

"Your message was very vague. What is it that you need, old friend?"

His blunt response and dismissal of the conversation regarding the woman seems forced. I'm not sure why he seems so touchy about discussing her further. He's the leader of the Authority. The most powerful man I know, human or otherwise. Not because his magic is so much greater than that of the others, but because of his connections.

If he wants something, he's given it without

question. I consider asking about the girl, but instead I move on to business. If he wanted to confide in me, he would. Besides, I hate to interfere. Still, the agreeable air seems dampened since she left and I don't care for the change.

"I wish you wouldn't call me that. I'm not nearly as old as you." He chuckles, knowing it's all in good humor. I almost smile at the sorcerer, but with the heavy situation weighing down on my shoulders, my body stays stiff. "Do you have somewhere more private we could speak?" He tilts his head and opens a drawer to pull out a notepad. A pen flies from the drawer and into his open hand before he scribbles something on a sheet of paper.

Away from meddling ears?

I nod my head once, maintaining eye contact while I set the teacup down on the desk.

"Of course. Let's head to the woods, shall we?" He snaps his fingers and the world blurs for only a moment before I'm sitting in the same comfortable chair, my hands still wrapped around the armrests, but in front of me is a babbling creek.

The morning light filters through the leaves onto the damp ground as a gentle wind passes. The shade of a large oak tree grants us privacy. It's a calm place that brings back memories.

I knew he'd bring us here. It's where we used to meet when I was younger. Back when I relied on him to get my footing as Alpha of my territory. Back when I struggled and worried I had made too many mistakes, and that I would fail my pack.

As I swallow down the recollections, a branch crunches under Alec's tread. "You didn't bring your chair," I comment. My head whirls for the span of a slow blink and then I feel settled once again. As if the world hadn't vanished and reappeared with the snap of his fingers.

"I have a feeling I'll be needing to stand." I get up from my seat to join him. We stand side by side watching the water flow over the small rocks. "Which one is it?"

"Which one?" I know what he's hinting at, but I'd rather he say it.

"Which one didn't you want to hear?" His hands are fisted and the balmy air around us stirs with irritation.

"Natalia." I answer honestly.

"Why is that?" His eyes darken, as does the sky. His anger isn't directed at me but I have to remind myself of that as I continue. I'm aware I'm one of a handful whom Alec shows this side to. The emotional, the part of him not ruled by logic. He doesn't need to hide in a cloud of comfort around me. He knows that. The sunless sky and chilled breeze are oddly comforting.

He echoes what stirs inside of me.

"What do you know about the blood you sell to the covens?" I'm relying on the last words of a dead man, but I have no doubt there's truth in what he said. And I trust Veronica's word.

"What blood?" Genuine confusion laces his question.

My fists clench at his ignorance. How the hell could they be conducting business right under his nose without him knowing? A tic in my jaw spasms with anger.

"The blood she's pushing on the covens." My hard words come out low, reflecting my disappointment with him. The clouds turn dark gray and thunder rumbles in the distance.

"She isn't—"

"She is," I say, cutting him off, and the seriousness of the accusation stretches between us.

He scowls and cracks his neck. The wind picks up

and the water of the creek seems to heat, the steam rising.

"How did she get that by you?" I stare at him with disbelief. Alec is not a force to be taunted and that's exactly what Natalia's doing. It's not wise of her, yet she's getting away with it.

"Things have been distracting me lately." He slowly regains his composure as he closes his eyes and controls his breathing. His fingers flex, the clouds slowly parting to reveal the sun again and the simmering water cools.

"Things? What kind of *things?*" He glances at me before settling his eyes back upon the free-flowing water. Whatever is bothering him needs to be taken care of immediately. His position as head of the Authority is one that many covet, and they would all kill to have his place. He's all too aware of that fact, as many have tried before.

"Another time for that tale, old friend." He's never hesitated before to confide in me. I square my shoulders as I face him and wait for his eyes to meet mine. A different anxiousness settles through me as doubt creeps into my thoughts.

"We are friends, aren't we, Alec?"

"We are." He smiles warmly at me. It eases my discomfort. "Friends and allies."

"You have many friends."

"No, I have few friends and many allies. They're quite different. You are a friend who happens to be my ally. I have few allies who happen to be my friends."

"That doesn't sound reassuring." He grunts a laugh before sitting on the grass, fiddling with his tie as he stares across the creek. I follow suit.

"It's not. Allies will only stand by you while you have something for them. While you hunger for the same."

"Out with it, Alec. I don't speak in code."

He smiles at my impatience. "Another time. Now, back to Natalia. You're sure of this?"

"I am. She seems to have the backing of the vampires in the Authority."

He nods in understanding.

"I figured; they all work together. It's no matter. They'll face the same consequence." Absently, he plucks two blades of grass and twirls them between his forefinger and thumb. I watch as they lengthen in his grasp, their pale green hue turning more vibrant as they grow.

"They're tainting the blood. I'm thinking they're

behind the abduction of the vampires who have gone missing recently. I'm sure they need test subjects."

His breathing stills and another round of thunder booms through the air. He crumples the grass in his fist and the stalks wither, turning brown, dying before my eyes. "Tainting it with what?"

"According to the shifter from Sarin's pack, Natalia made a deal with them. Drugs in exchange for control of Shadow Falls. She wants the blood bank so she can taint the blood she's forcing other vampires to drink. It's a new drug that voids their immortality."

Alec stares at me with disbelief evident in his expression. "I knew she was overstepping her boundaries with the vampires. But I had no idea she'd take it that far." His pale blue eyes search mine as he questions with a single breath, "Are you sure of this?"

"The shifter had nothing to gain and everything to lose by telling me this."

"We need to be certain, Devin. I can't get the backing of the rest of the Authority without irrefutable proof. This needs to be done quietly. No one can know. Not shifters, or vampires. And absolutely not the humans. There would be widespread panic." I already knew that would be his decision, but his sense of urgency regarding the matter is reassuring.

"I came prepared with a plan. Veronica's coven wants the blood bank, so we'll give it to them."

"And then?" His quizzical gaze meets mine.

"Then we'll have the ability to keep tabs on every move that is made."

Alec shakes his head. "This needs to happen quickly and quietly."

"I'll send her to her coven and gain permission for her to observe another town's bank. It'll be under the guise of seeing how things are done. A town where vampires have gone missing. Vince will go with her. Maybe he'll be able to tail them and sniff them out."

Alec nods once. "Do you need anything from me?"

"Not now, but when we're ready I'll need men to take them down."

"You won't have to worry about that. Keep me informed. When we have proof, you'll have the rest of the Authority on your side. It will be more than enough." His light blue eyes find mine and he smiles faintly before telling me, "She will pay greatly for this; I promise you that."

CHAPTER SEVEN

Veronica

THE KITCHEN APPEARS TO BE THE meeting place for the dogs. It seems they prefer this room to the others.

I glance at Dom and Caleb before quickly averting my eyes. My chest thumps and I struggle to restrain my heart from beating faster.

Embarrassment floods through me still.

I know they saw evidence that I'm not well. If I could go back to yesterday and hide it, I would. Instead I'm trapped here, on an estate run by were- wolves who are more than aware of my weakness.

Vince slips a hand down my arm, his thumb

rubbing soothing circles as if he knows exactly what I'm thinking. I offer him my hand over his, all the while pretending to listen to whatever joke Caleb is making.

I laugh when appropriate and do everything I can to avoid asking Vince what they're thinking. I already know; the sympathy is there every time Lizzie's eyes meet mine.

Focusing on keeping my breathing even, I slowly flex my hands under the table. My breath threatens to hitch and I start to slouch at the betrayal, but I keep my spine stiff and shoulders squared.

I wish he hadn't pinned me like that in front of them. I wish he wouldn't push me in private, let alone in front of them. I massage my wrists in my lap as anger consumes me. He fucking chained me.

The conversation continues without me. Devin needs to tell us what happened so I can get out of here. Back to the coven and back to safety.

Vince's large hand splays on my thigh; it's rough with calluses. My pup, my mate. My heart weakens at his touch.

The thought of leaving him behind has drifted to the forefront of my mind.

I know he only means to help me, but it's not

working. It makes me feel weak and helpless to be anywhere near him. I refuse to be either.

I've worked too damn hard for nearly two centuries to be made so vulnerable. He hasn't lived my life and he'll never know what I've endured. There's no fix or cure.

His simple mind thinks love alone will fix this. I pull away from him, but he grips me harder and turns his head to face me. His silver stare bores into me, but I refuse to look back. My fingers tingle with the itch to touch him; my body wants me to crawl into his lap, but I won't. I shift in my seat so I'm sitting sideways. The move breaks the contact his hand had on my thigh and settles my back to him.

I look toward Devin, defying my mate and my own needs. His exhale is long and slightly shaken. My heart sinks knowing I've hurt him. I don't care, though. He knows what he did. He can deal with the consequences. He knows the immense pain he caused me. What happened in the room was too fucking much for me to give him my love right now. There's nothing but silence and damage between us now. I should have known this would happen.

The last of the wolves, Jude, filters in and the atmosphere changes instantly.

"I want to make this fast and simple." Devin takes a long breath, both of his hands resting on the edge of the counter. His shoulders flex and Caleb stops mid-conversation. "Save your questions until the end." He looks pointedly at his mate and she huffs, not quite in annoyance, but then gives a short nod. She's quite brazen for a little human. I rub my wrists again and look down remembering yesterday morning. Remembering how weak I was yet again for sharing something so personal, too personal, with her. I have no idea what made me want to talk to her. I wish I hadn't. They know too much and I don't like it.

The name *Natalia* catches my attention and my eyes fly to meet Devin's as he speaks. "It appears Natalia and several of the vampires from the Authority are on a mission to eliminate any vampires opposing them."

A chill flows through me. I've suspected that for decades. I've felt she wished to reign over our species, to become the one true holder of authority. To have it spoken by someone else sparks a slight fear that my dreaded thoughts could become reality.

"What's the endgame there?" Dom asks.

"From what we've been told, Natalia wants to destroy their immortality," Devin replies.

A crease forms between my brow. *Destroy their immortality?* How is that even possible?

As if answering my unspoken question, Devin continues. "They're poisoning the blood from the donation centers and most likely the blood being sold to the covens." A mixture of fear and shock widens my eyes as I stare back at Devin's serious expression. His mate glances up at him, looking very much out of place.

It takes great effort to keep my lips shut tight although I want to bombard him with questions of how these allegations came to be. My gaze falls to Grace's laced fingers she's struggling to keep still as Devin delivers exactly what I want to know.

Her heart races and it doesn't escape me that she may feel what I feel in this moment.

"The shifter that attempted to take our mates told us they made a deal with a vampire. That they were going to cede control of Shadow Falls in exchange for a steady drug supply. Sarin's pack will deal with the consequences of their actions. But for now, Alec has asked for our help in proving the dead shifter's allegations are true.

"Veronica's coven wanted to make a deal with us to have a blood bank built in Shadow Falls." Devin's gaze settles on me and everyone else follows suit. "You'll go to your queen and let her know that we're willing to grant that request. No one will mention anything about what we've learned."

My lips part to object. I can't allow my coven to continue drinking tainted blood. Devin speaks before I can, though.

"No one, Veronica. Not one fucking word."

Vince stiffens beside me, but Devin doesn't hesitate to add, "If Natalia or any of the other vampires who are in on this find out that we know what they're up to, we'll be in danger. They will come to kill us and attack the allies we have within the Authority, or they will run. This is the best chance we have at stopping them."

Pressing my lips tightly together, I nod. I don't fucking like it, but I understand and I will obey because without his help, I have no way of knowing what is true and who to trust. Most don't adhere to the law anyway. I cling to that knowledge.

"What about Sarin's pack? Days have passed since the offering and we haven't heard anything," Caleb says.

"You'd think they'd give a shit that we killed four of their members." Jude's response to Caleb earns a nod from Dom.

Lev huffs and snorts before saying, "Yeah, right. Like they care."

"How are we going deal with them?" Dom's voice comes out hard.

"I should've ended him rather than let him run," Devin says, his brows pinching together as he drums his fingers along the table.

"What do we know of their pack?" I ask as I realize I don't know a single thing about the rival pack.

"They fled to a stronghold they have in the mountains. Maybe ten men remain; a few women too, I think," Devin tells us.

"They're weak now. We could easily take them," Caleb says.

Devin's fist slams on the granite countertops, forcing his mate to take a step back. "I will not risk our pack." He calms, softening his voice to add, "We cannot take on too much at once. Understood?"

The pack answers in unison, all but his mate, who peers up at him with uncertainty. Not weeks ago, this human had nothing to fear beyond mortal concerns. And now she's found herself on the brink of war, her fate tied to a mate who will lead us to it. Without looking back at her, Devin's hand reaches out for her and she takes his hand with both of hers.

"Jude, you'll scout out his pack. We don't know enough to go on the offensive. I want to know everything. Come back with intel and a plan of attack. We won't give them any mercy this time."

Jude acknowledges the command with "Yes, Alpha," and the attention turns to us.

"Vince and Veronica will go to her coven. Tell them I want to know how the blood banks are run and go to Still Waters. Three vampires have been abducted. Find them. I want to know everything that's going on. You have four days. No more than that. I also want you to take your fucking cell phone this time, Vince."

"You got it, Alpha," my mate says.

"What drug could possibly make us mortals?" I'm still reeling over this revelation. With all my thoughts running wild, I simply can't imagine it. In centuries there's never even been a whisper of magic or otherwise that could reverse our immortality.

"We don't know. The drug in the shifter we captured is an amphetamine called Captagon. It's highly addictive, plus it keeps them awake and energized." Devin's gaze finds Jude's as he adds, "That could be a problem for you. I expect to hear back from both you and Vince, every hour on the hour. Call Lev. If Lev doesn't hear from you, we'll come immediately. Is that clear?"

They answer in unison, but my question is still left unanswered. "What about the blood, what's the poison?" I can't imagine this drug actually existing.

"We don't know, Veronica. Keep her safe, Vincent."

"That goes without saying," Vince responds, his arm wrapping around my waist protectively. Although there's a warmth to his words and touch, I can't help the irritation. As if I can't keep myself safe. I'm one of the elites of the immortals. Shaking off the disagreeable thoughts I ponder the idea of this rumored drug's existence.

Something I could take that would rid me of this immortality; the thought lights a need deep within me I didn't know I had.

I could be a mortal again. I could be mortal like my mate.

A chill stiffens my bones. I used to dream of what my life would have been like if that day in the rainforest almost two hundred years ago had played out differently. With the knowledge I have now, I'm certain it would've been fucking awful. Still, I've often found myself envious of humans. A small curl to my lips reveals a single fang and I graze the tip of my tongue across the sharp point. If I drank this tainted blood, would I still have my fangs? How long would I live? Long enough to grow old with my mate? A comforting warmth surges through my body at the thought.

I turn slowly in my seat in his direction. He immediately grabs my chair to pull me closer to him. My stomach churns at how cold I was to him just moments ago and so many times in the past few days. He doesn't deserve how harsh I am toward him. I'm certain of this truth, yet I can't help my reaction when he pushes me like he has. I know he means well, but I don't care for it. If I were mortal, though … everything could change. This weight and burden could drift away.

I would give anything to grow old with him. Could I bear children for him? There's no doubt in my mind that I would trade my immortality to have a child. I've lived long enough and experienced more than most would ever dream of. But the pull between Vince and me … this desire to carry a child, perhaps a wolf like him … I would give anything, drink anything. The temptation weighs heavy on my heart. I need to learn more of this drug. If it's true, if I could be mortal again, I would sacrifice everything to have it.

CHAPTER EIGHT

Grace

"**H**OW DO YOU KNOW YOU'RE pregnant? It's way too early to tell, isn't it?" I still can't wrap my head around the idea that Lizzie could be pregnant. That she even said it.

There's just no way to know that so quickly. It's not possible.

"Dom and Caleb are convinced. They said they can smell it."

"They can smell it?" My nose wrinkles slightly and I take in the sight of my best friend sitting at the end of the counter. In gray sweats and an oversized white T-shirt that I think is Caleb's, she's relaxed as can be as she drops this bombshell.

"They're sure?"

"It's too early for it to be certain, but that's what they said." Pulling the sleeves of my cream sweater over my hands, I keep my fingers tucked inside so I stop picking at the small tear in my jeans. Is she really pregnant? Everything has been too much too fast. I don't understand why she isn't freaking out right now.

"I don't feel any different. I'm just telling you what they said." She shrugs.

Lizzie pops a spoonful of yogurt into her mouth and closes her eyes before she tells me, "I fucking love strawberry yogurt. How come we never bought this before?"

I smile at her goofiness, although it's subdued. Seriously, it's just yogurt. "Didn't know you liked it." Shifting slightly on the barstool, I debate on getting into such a heavy topic, but it's too important not to. "Are you happy?"

Her bright eyes soften as she readjusts her stool and the legs drag on the floor. She puts her hand out on the table, palm up. I put my hand in hers and she squeezes in response. "Happier than I've ever been." Her reassuring words make my whole body relax.

"Are you really pregnant?" I can't fathom that in only days she knows she's pregnant. She shrugs her shoulders and goes back to scraping the plastic cup with her spoon, trying to get out as much as possible.

"They said between the two of them, there's no way they weren't going to knock me up during this last heat." She giggles into her cup, now licking the sides of it since the spoon isn't effective enough. I shake my head and hop off my perch to grab her another from the fridge.

"You're ready to be a mom?"

She smiles as she catches the new cup I toss at her. "I can't fucking wait, Grace. Can you just imagine it? A little baby, cooing at us, snuggling into my arms."

"They scream too, you know? And poop a lot." She laughs at my blunt statement and nods her head.

"Yeah, I know. They have their moments. But it's all worth it. All the late nights of them wanting to be held. When they're gone, I'll miss them. I may be irritated when they cry every time I put them down, but when they're older, I'll wish they'd let me hold them again."

I vaguely wonder if focusing on a baby is a way for her to cope with how different our lives are now.

I wonder if it's all moving too fast. I worry for her, but I bite my tongue.

It's not my place and I'll stand with her through anything.

"It's not abnormal, Grace," Lizzie says softly, as if she knows exactly what I'm thinking. "When mates meet and the heat happens … this is what is expected."

She offers me a small smile as she pats my hand. "I've always wanted to be a mom, and I love my mates, truly. Both of them. Even if it's all too fast and there's so much to learn. When I was little, this was my happily ever after. Before … everything else. This was all I wanted."

Her doe eyes brim with tears and I wrap my arms around her in concern. "Fuck, I'm so damn hormonal, Grace." She lets out a sad laugh while tears slip down her cheeks. Wiping them away, she pulls back to tell me, "I don't just want a little baby; I want a family." She leans back farther, dropping her spoon and unopened yogurt into her lap. "I *have* a family."

"You do," I whisper, only just now realizing what she must be feeling. Reconciling her past and present, accepting love, and finally knowing she's safe. They'll protect her from everything.

"They love me so much and I love them too."

"Damn, girl," I joke to lighten the mood as she attempts to gather her composure, "you're definitely pregnant. All emotional." She laughs and pulls her legs into her chest, wiping her eyes.

"I hope I am." Her happiness makes me question my decision to wait. The way she's come round to them makes me wonder if I should do the same with Devin.

The thought of Lizzie holding a baby suddenly sends all sorts of emotions shooting through me, jealousy being the most prominent. It catches me off guard. I'm not a jealous person, and especially not of Lizzie. I want her to have happiness. It's quiet for a moment as I stand up, wanting to shake all of this off.

I shuffle to the fridge to find something to eat while I question my feelings. "What do you think it'll be like?"

"Having a baby?" Her eyes catch mine briefly before I look into the freezer.

"Yeah."

"Heaven. Well, sometimes heaven, sometimes hell. But it's all a phase and it will be worth the hard times."

"It's so much responsibility, so life changing." I snort at my own words. Everything has been so fucking life changing. It seems like every day there's something new, yet Devin is unaffected. Is this world of chaos and danger my normal now?

"It is, but I've always wanted a big family."

"Really?" Surprise coats the single word. "I never knew that."

She nods as I shut the fridge, a package of yogurt in my hand. She says, "I never really talked about it. It's not like I'd ever let a guy near me so …" She breathes deep before tossing the cup at the trash can and missing. "Crap." Getting up, she walks over to clean up her mess.

"Is that why?" I question as I lean against the counter.

"Why what?"

"Why you never dated anyone?" I feel like a shit friend for not knowing any of this before. She's always been flirtatious but that's as far as things went. To be honest, none of the guys we would hang around with ever seemed like they were good enough for her, so I never questioned her not getting serious with anyone.

"I don't know. I just buried it all and tried not to think about it." She's pitching the cup in the trash; this time it makes it. "You know, I never thought I'd have kids. Since I'm latent, I didn't know if I could risk trying to have a family. What if I settled for some guy back in Shadow Falls? Obviously he would've been human. I peel back the lid slowly, taking my time and letting Lizzie say whatever's on her mind.

"If I settled down with some guy, I never could've told him about what I am. Heck … I couldn't even tell you. And then if we had a baby, and that baby was a werewolf …" She shakes her head as she trails off, the rose gold and moonstone earrings I gifted her gently chiming. Lizzie retakes her seat and spins on her stool. She bites her lip, obviously thinking about something. Finally she stops and looks at me as I take the seat next to her. "I always wanted to tell you, but I just couldn't. I didn't want to believe it was true. Some days I'd actually convince myself it was just a nightmare. It was so much easier living like that." She leans in and lays her head on my shoulder. "You're not mad at me, are you?"

Resting my head on top of hers, I answer honestly, "I could never be mad at you, babe. Besides, I knew you went through something and when you were ready, you'd tell me."

"I didn't think I would have ever been ready, though. I never wanted to deal with it, you know?"

She leans back to look me in the eyes while I swirl the spoon in yogurt I don't even want to eat.

Setting it down on the counter with finality I nod slightly and tell her, "I know. I really do get it. You don't have to be worried about me. You know I still love you."

"I love you too." She kisses my cheek before going back to spinning on her seat.

All this heavy talk is making a lump form in my throat. My whole world is nothing like it was before. It's as if I'm living in a completely different reality and so much is out of my control.

I decide to change the subject to something I've been wondering about and something I'm certain Lizzie will want to hash out. "Are werewolf babies born human, or like …" I trail off as I think about getting pregnant with Devin's *pups*.

"Do you remember in biology when we talked about the difference between altricial and whatever the fuck the other word is?"

I just blink at her before stating flatly, "I fucking hated bio." My comment grants me a belly laugh from Lizzie that lights up her face and I'm forced to smile in return.

When she recovers, she starts one of her little tidbit tangents she's known for.

"Some babies are born and they're completely dependent on their mother, like humans and dogs, whereas other species give birth and the babies go on their merry way, fully independent, like"—she scrunches her nose in thought—"like sharks, I think."

"You're such a dork." My cheeks hurt from grinning at her. My best friend appears to be back to her usual happy-go-lucky self. For a moment, it all feels normal. For a moment, the smallest moment, I forget everything has changed.

"The first one is called altricial and that's what werewolves are."

"That doesn't really answer my question."

She stares blankly at me. How does she not get this?

"So your baby may be a werewolf, or definitely will be? And … importantly, do they look like human when they're born or …" I let the question hang between us, not wanting to imagine the alternative.

Her sarcastic smirk tells me she pities me for my complete lack of knowledge. "This form, as humans, is how they're delivered." I let out a deep breath at that statement. Her next, though, has me tensing right back up. "They'll be werewolf. So will yours, by the way." Lizzie raises her eyebrows at me before continuing. "I just don't know if they'll be latent like me or if they'll be normal."

Latent. My heart sinks as I watch her shoulders hunch. I don't fucking like her getting down on herself. "But you said you felt her, right? Your wolf?"

"Just the once since we've been here. I don't know why she left me." Her somber statement dampens her mood as she spins slowly on the stool.

"What brought her back?" Lizzie blushes at my question, which makes me really want to know what happened. Yes! This is a much better conversation to have. My cheeks burn and I lean in to whisper, "Was it the sex?"

She bites her lip again, looking shy. It's an odd look for her to give me when she tells me, "We didn't have sex, just did other stuff." She shakes her head and composes herself. "But we've had sex since then and she didn't come back. Unless—" Her eyes brighten and she takes a quick inhale.

"What? What was it that brought her back?" I love the hopeful light in her blue eyes.

"Caleb punished me with a belt—"

"What the fuck!" I jump out of my seat, causing it

to fly backward and crash on the tile floor. *Punished?* My head spins as the word registers.

Every hair on my body stands on end as adrenaline has me seeing nearly red.

I practically scream as my body burns with anger. "I'll fucking kill him. Where the fuck is Dom?" My heart races as my hands ball into tight fists at my sides. *How the fuck could he hit her?*

"Knock it off, Grace!" Lizzie's quick to tug at my arm while scowling. "And shut your mouth about Dom." She hushes me with a tone I'm not used to and a hurt in her doe eyes that I don't understand. "He didn't do a damn thing to me." I step back, the wind taken out of my sails by her offended reaction.

"He hit you." Staring at her wide eyed with disbelief, I don't understand how she could possibly be defending him.

"First of all, Dom has never laid a finger on me." Her voice cracks as she speaks. "Dom loves me and so does Caleb. Caleb's the one who used a belt to get me to open up to him. And I fucking loved it." She points her finger at me and pushes out each choked-up word with a tone that brooks no disagreement. "You better not fucking judge me for it, Grace."

"I—" I don't know what to say. A numbness of

regret runs through me. "I had no right to react that way. I'm sorry. I'm sorry, Lizzie." Putting my hands up in surrender, I walk toward her. My best friend is practically shaking with emotion. "I'm so sorry, babe, it was wrong of me to jump to conclusions." She leans into me for a hug.

"Please don't think badly of me. Don't hold it against him," she says softly. Lizzie pulls back with her hands on my shoulders and says, "Tell me you won't think badly of him. Please." My lips part, although I'm somehow able to hold my tongue. He hit her. He punished her.

"You liked it?" She nods her head and brushes the tears away with the back of her hand. "A belt?" She blushes again, bright red this time.

"I swear, Grace. It was … kinky and I loved it."

"Okay." I try to imagine it and then regret it. "If you're happy, then I'm happy." Taking a deep breath, I look right into those baby blue eyes of hers when I tell her, "But if either of them hurts you, you know you can tell me, right?"

"It's a good hurt." Her cheeks flush beet red before she gives me a hug as if to end the conversation there. "I love them so damn much. I'm so fucking happy."

To each their own, I suppose. I don't know if I'll

ever look at Caleb the same again. Between the pair of her mates there's no way I'd have guessed it was Caleb who'd be into that. An odd feeling comes over me as a weight seems to lift off my chest. I glance at my best friend, so happy and at peace with everything. I feel like I can let go, like for the first time in our lives, she doesn't need me. She has her mates now. Walking past her to pick up my fallen stool, Lizzie gasps and touches her chest.

"Lizzie?" The chair drops back to the floor at the sight of her shocked expression and her hand clutching her shirt.

"I feel my wolf, Grace. I feel her!" Staring at Lizzie, I'm frozen in place.

"What should I do?" I'd do anything for her, but I have no idea how to help her or what to do.

"I don't know. I don't know. I'm so scared she's going to leave me." Tears well in her eyes again. She rubs her chest before whispering, "Please don't leave me."

CHAPTER NINE

Vince

I'VE NEVER BEEN AFRAID OF VAMPIRES. NEVER in my whole life have I even bothered with the thought of fearing bloodsuckers.

But holy fuck. Walking into the den of Veronica's coven, surrounded by vampires on all sides, I'd be lying if I said there wasn't a cold prick traveling down my spine and eliciting a hint of fear.

Veronica is the first vampire I've met who I've seen as more than an enemy. She's the first I've been able to interact with beyond strategizing about defense and offense. I've seen them before, of course, from the Authority, whenever Devin invited them into our estate, onto our territory. I've killed them when necessary. I've never had to question what would happen if they attacked. Our pack would have demolished them.

There is no pack with me now, though. On their turf and highly outnumbered, I'm not naive enough to think I stand a chance against them. If they decided I was their prey tonight, there isn't a thing I could do to win a fight against the coven.

Acutely aware of such facts, I wrap my arm casually around Veronica's waist. I may be humbled by the terrifying thought, but I'm sure as shit not going to let them know. In my periphery, I keep tabs on them watching me.

Swallowing thickly, I keep my pace even with Veronica's. The click of her heels is muted as she walks, the sound absorbed by the hardened earth.

Why the fuck do they live underground? They're wealthy beyond belief.

They've had hundreds of years to acquire riches and properties. It's known as fact among supernaturals that vampires are stacked with cash. They could afford to build mansions above ground where no sunlight would ever touch them. Yet they live in a fucking cave.

As I lick my lips, the salty air from the damp walls settles on the tip of my tongue. It's a refreshing taste. If I closed my eyes I could almost picture myself on a beach, but it's far too cold.

Again, I'm not a bitch, but why live like this when you could live anywhere? Fucking stupid, if you ask me. Of course, if they're going for intimidating, then they hit that nail on the fucking head. With only torches lining the pitch-black passageway, secured in sconces placed every few feet along the rock walls, it's dark for those whose sight is weak. Realizing I can see better than any of them puts a smirk on my lips.

A relatively large form passes in front of us down another dreary, fire-lit hall; he's a few inches shorter than me and only wearing a pair of white linen pants. His bare feet and chest reflect the light off his pale skin. I catch his scent and the sight of him clearly: human.

My forehead pinches in confusion for only a moment before I see the small scars along his neck. They form an interesting overlapping pattern, like the scales of a dragon. It must've taken hundreds of bites over a long period of time to make that kind of rough scar on the thin skin of his neck. They're only in a small patch on the right side. I lose sight of him as he walks farther through the passage and we continue straight ahead. With a glance down, I note that Veronica doesn't react.

The tunnel appears to end in front of us. No fire on the walls is present to light the path. It only takes a moment to spot the thick, dark red curtains pulled shut that are blocking our way. Veronica reaches forward, drawing one curtain aside. I take the other heavy panel and pull it back much farther than she can, then gesture for her to take the lead. She tries to hide it, but I see her small, satisfied smirk she immediately represses.

My chest constricts. I don't know whether we're okay or not. She's barely spoken to me since I let her off the bed. She's been glacial to me, icing me out. She hasn't tried to boss me around or even called me pup. Nothing. She's given me very little of her attention. She shies away from any physical contact between us. At least she's accepting my touch now that we're in her territory.

What worries me is that I don't know how I'll react if she continues to ignore me while we're here. Where I have no one but her. There's only so much I can hide and my wolf yearns for her touch and acceptance. Brushing off the unwanted feelings, I remind myself she's been more receptive since we left the estate. She's not giving me her full attention, but she's not ignoring me either.

At the thought, her hand briefly brushes against mine. As if she can perceive I need the reassurance. Veronica makes me weak. I would drop to my knees, begging for her to command me if that would ease the tension between us. If she told me to submit to her this very moment, I wouldn't hesitate.

She hasn't told me shit, though. Not a single word.

I'm not sure if she'll ever trust me. What little trust she had in me seems to have been diminished by me chaining her to the bed. It was only meant to help; to show her she didn't have any reason to fear me or my touch. That I would always be hers even if she had no physical control of me. It didn't work. I fucking failed her.

Again.

My chest constricts and my heart skips a beat momentarily. Nearly forgetting where we are, I remind myself to be more mindful of their hearing. Fuck.

After a minute, I shake it off. I *will* heal her. I will help my mate learn to trust me. It's going to take time and I need to accept that. Exhaling a long breath causes Veronica to take a peek at me. Her gorgeous dark eyes pierce through me, not hiding her concern.

Even if she hates herself for it, she cares for me. I know she does.

I smile down at her. Everything in me yearns to kiss her, but I hold myself back. I won't be able to contain myself if she rejects me. And we're in her territory, not mine. I repress the low growl from my wolf. He wants her. I haven't had her since the claiming and that didn't go well. I need to feel her body against mine. I need to give her pleasure and hear her moans of approval. Tightening my arm around her waist brings her closer to me. She stiffens slightly at first, which puts my wolf on high alert, but then she relaxes against me. He's still not happy. He paces restlessly inside me, knowing something's wrong, just not knowing what.

My focus leaves me as I sense a flood of warmth in front of me. Again the tunnel seems to end, but as I expect, thick curtains cut off the passage. I pull at the dark fabric to reveal a brightly lit room. Veronica doesn't hesitate to walk into the luxurious space and I follow her lead. She leaves my hold, but I'm quick to pull her ass back to me. She's mine. And all these fuckers are going to see that.

Apart from a raised brow, she doesn't object to my touch. *Good girl.*

The vast room is more of what I expected to see from her queen and ancient coven. The walls and ceiling are covered in ornate designs. Breathing in deep, I take in the scent of minerals. Gold. It's painted in gold. A closer look at the rough rock walls reveals luxury and decadence beyond belief. The masterful artistry on display must have taken decades to create. I have to squint to make out the hundreds of small fires blending together across the expansive space to make a literal wall of fire. The tone-on-tone metallic paint reflects the flames to the point where it nearly pains my eyes to stare straight ahead. Most of the furniture in the room appears ancient; the seats are intricately carved pieces lined with bloodred velvet fabric. It's completely at odds with the modern, clear acrylic table in the very center of the room.

The seat at the head of the table is taken by a tall, pale woman with smooth skin and black silky hair down to her small waist. Her sharp red nail pierces into her lip as her dark eyes find us. She rises in a blur of motion but then takes a small, slow step forward, making the black jewels adorning her dress clink together as she walks. She reeks of wealth and power.

Her nearly black eyes have a youthful shine although I know better.

The other vampires in the room hardly take notice of our entry. But the humans, all wearing the same pants or halter dresses of white linen, take an obvious interest in our presence. All look to us but a single woman lying still on a plush white hide off to the right side of the room. For a moment I tense, thinking the human is dead. But the air carries no scent of decay. I watch her chest gently rise and fall. Fresh, open wounds on her neck indicate someone drank from her recently, but she's alone on the floor. My gut twists with the thought that the humans are here against their will, present only to satisfy the thirst of the vamps. The delight evident in the sets of eyes following our movement begs to differ with my assumption. I would quietly ask Veronica for confirmation, but vampires are known for their ability to hear at great distances.

My curiosity will have to wait.

The seductive voice of the black-eyed queen echoes gently off of the walls. "Veronica, my darling. You've brought a guest?"

A devious smile brightens Veronica's crimson lips. The firelight illuminates her tan skin. She's breathtaking in this lighting, glowing with a golden sheen. My pulse races and desire threatens to consume me. My gorgeous mate is in her element and she thrives here. I can feel her strength through our bond; I practically see her transform into the fierce warrior I met in the alley.

Before I claimed her.

Before I broke her. I shake off the thought. No, I'm *healing* her. She's hurting. Her ability to hide her pain is extraordinary. My eyes travel along her beautiful face, alight with mischief and seduction.

"A guest, or a snack?" a pale man with the same dark eyes says. In less time than it takes to blink, he makes his way across the room to stand in front of me. I swallow thickly, not letting their speed and number cause any more alarm than the initial shock. His clothes and the way his short blond hair is styled nearly make him look human. But his eyes give away his dependency on consuming blood.

"Braeden, you know I don't share." Veronica's voice is playful as she turns her back on her coven to pat the center of my chest. Her head tilts up at me and I don't waste a second to bend down and give her a small kiss on the lips. I keep my eyes closed longer than necessary, sending a clear sign to them that I don't fear their presence. They're no threat to me. At least that's what my actions suggest.

She waits until I open my eyes and I'm caught in her gaze for only a moment as she peers back up at me. There's something there, something between us, but it's quickly forgotten.

Veronica spins to face them, causing her leather skirt to flare around her. "I've found a mate, Adreana. I'll be staying with him for a while." A tic in my jaw spasms and my eyes harden on her back. *A while?* My stomach sinks as I realize the full weight of her words. My life span will be a blip in her existence.

"Of course, darling. Of course." The queen's eyes travel down my body with appreciation. I don't care for it. "So he's yours alone?"

Veronica nods her head slightly before walking past the table to a chaise longue in the corner of the room, extremely close to the wall of fire. "Funny that fate should give me a mate. Don't you think so, my queen?"

"It's odd. It's not completely unheard of, although I thought they were just rumors before."

Braeden appears by Veronica's side, but sits on the ground and stares at the fire with his knees pulled into his chest. He's so motionless he looks like he's made of stone. Veronica shifts her long legs onto the sofa in a very seductive move and pats the seat between her legs. I move deliberately with a casual pace and take my seat, a smirk begging to form on my lips. Her right calf rests on my thigh as her queen stalks toward us.

"What are the rumors, Adreana? I've no memory of a pairing like ours." My thumb rubs small circles on the inside of my mate's knee. She's relaxed and at peace, although it seems false. My eyes linger on her face, her expression one of disinterest; however, she's obviously curious. Her queen sits to my left and I lean back to give the two women an easy view of each other. I feel very much out of place in the quiet room, but I continue to follow Veronica's lead. I'd much rather have her queen's approval as quickly as possible to go to Still Waters and stake out the blood bank, but Veronica doesn't appear to be in any rush.

"I couldn't tell you, my dear. There was word that a vampire had mated with a wolf, and that was all to be said. I'm not sure he ever returned." Adreana's eyes focus on my fingers stroking the inside of Veronica's knee before traveling to her neck. "And you let him claim you, I see. Rather barbaric, wouldn't you agree." I don't let her words affect me in the least as I hold the queen's gaze. Veronica lets out a huff of a small laugh.

"It was quite primitive, but it suited my taste."

"If you say so. And what of the Alpha, is he willing to negotiate? I'm hoping this mating benefited us." Her voice rises toward the end.

"It did, my queen. Devin is willing to give us the bank and allow our control without any interference."

The queen laughs in obvious amusement, then says, "You toy with me, darling?"

Veronica's eyes spark with delight at her queen's approval. "I'd never. He of course desires a plan and would like my mate to receive information from a successful territory. He chose Still Waters. We're planning on taking our leave this evening, I believe."

"I see." The queen sighs and leans deep into the chaise, beckoning an onlooking human to come to her. The man smiles and rises slowly, kneeling in front of her, waiting for her next command. She gently runs her fingers through his thick brown hair.

We sit in silence for a moment. Braeden seems to grow bored and stands, walking to the young woman lying on the plush rug. He squats in front of her and runs his fingers down her chin. "Come, pet."

"I'm tired … You drank so much." She barely breathes the words as she leans into his touch. He chuckles deep and low.

"You need to sleep; would you prefer the floor to my bed?" His voice is full of humor.

"Your bed, please."

He lifts her in his arms as though she weighs nothing and saunters easily out of the room.

"And what do the Alpha and his pack think of the law? Are you expected to only drink from your mate?" The queen's alluring voice brings my eyes to hers, although she's not looking in our direction whatsoever. Her focus is on the man waiting patiently on his knees in front of her.

Veronica smiles easily and says, "He holds the same opinion as I." Her hand finds mine and she brings my fingers to her mouth to suck. My dick instantly hardens. With a quick inhale, I suppress my groan and the need to let my head fall back. The room's sweet smell and the heat of the fire add to the seductive quality of the unnaturally beautiful vampires. "My mate enjoys my touch and I continue to drink from him."

Although her voice is even, the queen's next statement holds a viciousness that's unexpected. "Do you think of me as a hypocritical bitch? Or a coward for bowing to Natalia's demand?"

Veronica sits up abruptly, her speed shocking me

for a moment. She bows her head slightly with her lips grazing my knee. "Neither, my queen," she says and her softly spoken words tickle my knee.

"Up." Adreana rests her hand on Veronica's shoulder, and in turn my mate's dark eyes find her queen's. "I'm itching for a war, darling."

"We would stand at your side, if you so desired." My spine stiffens at the turn of the conversation.

This will all be taken care of shortly. The coven would only interfere. I keep my lips pressed tight and rest my hand lightly on Veronica's back, rubbing soothing circles. Her eyes close briefly at my touch, making my wolf pant with longing.

"For now, we'll build the bank. Her presence here will not be tolerated. Not after what she did to Stephan."

For the first time, I turn and look the queen in the eyes. "My Alpha was not pleased to hear what Natalia has done. He sends his sincere condolences."

Her dark eyes search mine for a long moment before she finally speaks. "Well thank you, my dearest wolf. Please send him my regards." Her hand stops in the human's hair and the lack of her touch has him seeking out her gaze. "Would you like me to drink from you, Jaret?"

"Please, my queen." His tone is deferential, but his green eyes practically beg her.

"Come." In a blur that leaves a gentle breeze in her wake, suddenly the queen is standing by the entrance. She passes through the heavy velvet curtains without a single glance over her shoulder as the human quickly follows her path. It's an abrupt end to the conversation to say the least.

"I need to pack, pup." The use of Veronica's pet name for me stirs my dick. My lips lift into a grin as she leans in for a kiss.

"Yes, Mistress." I feel her smile against my lips. Something deep inside me twists, knowing I'm playing into her hand. I'll give her this for now. A give-and-take of sorts. "When we get home, I want you chained again." My words turn the quiet room silent and I feel several pairs of dark eyes boring into me. My mate stiffens, but only for a moment. She leans back and stands.

"When we get back. Until then …" Her words are left hanging in the air as she walks toward the exit. The blazing heat from the fire quickly fades, leaving me cold in its absence. I pull her frame into my chest and kiss the crook of her neck.

"I love you." Those eyes bore into me again as she

turns in my embrace. Her hand rests on the center of my chest. Her lips part and close before her dark eyes find mine.

"I love you too, Vince," she says, barely speaking the words loud enough for me to hear. Her soft, plump lips press against mine in a chaste kiss. She hums her appreciation and turns, straightening her back and lifting her chin. Her strong voice returns. "Now come, pup; we're going to be late." My lips curl in a grin as I follow my mate down the dark, damp hall.

CHAPTER TEN

Vince

It's easy enough to catch the scent of the vampires among the humans. Special contacts disguise their eyes and they're dressed in the latest fashion trends unlike Veronica's coven, allowing them to blend into their surroundings. Even so, there are two I spot immediately. One near the entrance, appearing preoccupied at a desk as his fingers click along a keyboard. He pauses momentarily when we enter, but doesn't seem to care enough to fully stop his work. The other I scent is somewhere down the hall.

The building on the whole is small and sterile.

As we enter, I calculate every escape route available should we need one. In front of us are several couches and a small TV on the wall, playing some sort of animated comedy. There are three humans seated in the waiting room and I can smell blood being drawn from at least one more somewhere. I whisper softly to Veronica at the shell of her ear, "I thought the Authority only allowed humans to work the building and deliver the blood?" From what I know of their laws, there shouldn't be any vampires here at all.

"That was before vampires started going missing. They used to come alone once a day to pick up the blood and that was all. Now they have two in place at all times, although they aren't to present themselves as anything other than human." I grunt, taking in her words. A little warning would have been nice.

"Do you two have an appointment or are you walk-ins?" a peppy blond woman asks from the front desk. Her eyes drift down my body slowly as she licks her lower lip and clenches her thighs far too noticeably. Veronica surprises me by gripping my hand in a possessive response.

I must admit, her claiming me in such a subtle and human way is more than attractive. I squeeze her hand in return, reveling in the contact.

"Neither. We're here to take a look around, thanks." Her short dismissal nearly makes me laugh as she tugs me along.

"You're here for the tour?" The first vampire I made out rises and strides over, extending his hand for me to shake. Making eye contact, I grip him firmly. His gaze darts to Veronica's. Not that his coworker notices, but subtle clues indicate he's surprised; I'm guessing he didn't realize I was a werewolf. I grin at him before releasing his hand.

"Are you going to show us around or what?" I comment casually, still grinning.

He recovers quickly and says, "Right this way, miss …?"

"Mrs." Veronica's response makes me snort a laugh. "Please call me by my first name, Veronica. I believe Melinda arranged the appointment." There's slight tension between the two but it's quickly eased.

He gives her a small smile while leading us through the hall. His demeanor turns professional as a short woman leaves the small room to our right with an adhesive bandage on her arm, obviously having just given blood. "Have a wonderful day," he tells her.

"You too," she replies. The woman leaves without even glancing in our direction.

The vampire's fangs aren't visible at all. He's obviously practiced a smile that hides them. I wonder how long he's hidden here among them and what he's heard. Humans have always left me curious. With my new mate, however, vampires may just become my new obsession.

"After you." He motions us into a small room, his button-down shirt shifting slightly as he does and the scent of vampire permeates the air. There's a simple desk with a computer that looks old as shit sitting in the corner. Behind it are a swivel chair and a cabinet housing a variety of equipment. A medical waste bin sits in one corner. Overall, everything looks very simple and not nearly as high tech as I was expecting.

"It's a bit outdated, isn't it?" I quirk a brow at the vampire and he smiles, revealing a bit of his fangs. With no humans around, he freely drops the act.

"Humans get suspicious of wealth."

I nod at his admission. "Makes sense."

Veronica takes the lead, asking him, "What changes have been made since the abductions? We want to know the ins and outs of operations. If you could also explain how vampires managed to disappear in human territory, I would appreciate that information as well."

Her nose wrinkles at the modest surroundings as she paces to the chair with her arms crossed listening to the vampire's response.

"Melinda said a member of Adreana's coven would be here. She didn't say anything about a wolf."

In a blur, she's beside me. "He's with me." With a smirk, she trails her nails along my arm. The move elicits a low growl of approval for the public display of affection.

"Is your Alpha open to relations with other covens?" His question is directed at me, although he noticeably swallows and doesn't make eye contact.

"No. We are willing to appease my mate's queen. That is all."

"I see. How … unusual." The vampire eyes Veronica's neck, lingering on my mark.

"I asked about the changes to protocol?" Veronica says coolly.

"As you can see, we have two of us on guard now. At all times. The three who were abducted were alone when it happened. Since then, we haven't allowed the rogue vampires a chance to take anyone else."

"Rogue vampires?" My hackles raise.

"It had to be other vampires." There's a pause and Veronica's gaze narrows. "There's no way it could've been anyone else. Humans wouldn't dare even if they had the ability to kidnap vampires. The wolves here in Still Waters respect our treaties. Our coven showed the security footage to the Authority. They haven't found anything yet."

"Who was it from the Authority that you spoke with?" My voice comes out hard and his gaze shifts from Veronica to me, back to her and then settles on me once again.

"I'm not sure. It was between them and my queen." He clasps his hands in front of him, not hiding his unease at my presence.

"It's no matter. Do you know why your queen is convinced it was vampires?"

He nods his head at Veronica's question, much more comfortable addressing her. It's probably better that way. Vampires naturally fear my kind and it should stay that way. "We could clearly see the vision of a running vampire. But only for a moment on the screen before Joshua left the property."

"So he was lured away by a vampire?"

"We have no doubt." With a curt nod, his voice is firm. "However, you have nothing to worry about. Although the Authority hasn't made any arrests, we haven't seen any strange activity since we've placed two of us on the property at all times. It is safe and operations have gone seamlessly since then."

"So you simply collect the blood and bring it back to your coven?"

"Yes. Nothing less and nothing more. I'm certain you won't encounter any problems." My eyes search the room for anything amiss. Devin's convinced they're poisoning the blood somehow. My eyes narrow as they zero in on the boxes behind the door.

"Where do you get your equipment?" I ask.

"The Authority sets you up with everything you need to start. It's cheaper than buying everything separately from the humans. And this way we avoid doing any more activity with them than we have to."

"Well, that's very convenient." Veronica voices my own thoughts. If I had to guess, I'd say the blood bags used to collect donations are what's poisoned; maybe they lace the plastic lining.

But what the hell do I know? We're going to have to test the materials after we place an order.

"Do you drink it?" I can't help but to ask if for no other reason than curiosity. A part of me feels complicit for knowing these vampires could be consuming drugs without knowing. It's obvious that Veronica's coven isn't adhering to the law, but how many other covens are as lenient as hers?

His eyes dart between the two of us before he replies, "Of course I do. It's law."

Veronica laughs a sweet, low seductive sound while trailing her fingers down my neck and resting them in the dip of my collarbone. "I prefer sweeter tastes."

"Wolves are sweeter?" His brows raise as he regards my wrists and neck curiously. The way his gaze lingers makes me think he must be hungry. Maybe they are only drinking what's been donated. When his eyes reach my hard stare, he flinches.

"I think we're good here," I state bluntly. I don't appreciate being looked at like I'm a fucking meal. Not by him anyway.

With a soft hum of agreement, Veronica laces her fingers between mine, peering up at me. The male vampire is quick to look away.

I lead Veronica out, loving that she holds on to my hand without hesitation.

Still, I can't help feeling a twisting knot deep in my gut. I just don't feel right. We haven't been intimate since the offering. My wolf isn't happy. My balls aren't either. Every few hours I'm rock hard for her and I'm going to need a release soon. Preferably before I lose my damn mind.

As we walk down the narrow hall, the scents mingle and that unsettled feeling turns into something else. "Let me do a lap and try to catch the scent."

Veronica pauses in the middle of the hall with me, the vampire to our backs. "Do you think you'll find anything?"

I shrug and tell her, "Possibly. A vampire's scent is much different from a human's."

"Oh," she says and purses her lips, "and what is it that we smell like?"

"More metallic and salty." That's the best response I can come up with. It's hard to describe their smell.

She huffs in distaste and says, "So you're saying I smell like a rock."

"No, you smell like honey and jasmine." I lean in close to her ear, backing her body against the handrail, then tell her, "You taste like them too." Heat dances between us instantly and she sucks in a breath, taken aback and very much weak for me. She lets her head fall back, which gives me a clear view of my mark on her. I bend down to kiss it, but she seems to realize my intention and pushes away from me. That twisting sickness in my stomach roils.

"Do a lap and see if you can smell anything." She maneuvers her way out of my hold and it takes everything in me not to react. Not to hold her still, press her against the wall and take her lips with mine. I watch her walk away from me, staying as still as I can.

Taking one deep breath and then another, my tense muscles relax. At least she's found her strength and is giving me orders again.

I follow her out of the blood bank walking a step or two behind. When she stops at the car and turns to face me, I step into her space. It fucking kills me when she stiffens as I cage her body in. Her eyes flash with fear, and then defiance as they narrow at me. She has no reason for either reaction.

I lean down and breathe in her sweet honey scent before kissing her neck. If I want to kiss my mark on her, I'm going to fucking kiss it. I leave an open-mouthed kiss exactly where I want it and breathe into her neck, "My Mistress."

As I pull back, she doesn't react. There's a sadness in her eyes, followed by nothing. In a blink, nothing. It guts me.

How have we taken such a huge step back in our relationship? It was so fucking easy, so damn good before. My fists clench as I leave her and head for the back of the building, the thin skin over my knuckles going taut and turning white. My jog turns into a sprint. How the hell did I mess this up so fucking bad?

No. My fist pounds against the dumpster as I near the back exit, leaving a massive dent in the side. I look around and release the breath I was holding when I see that no one saw my outburst. I need to check my anger before it creates more trouble.

I didn't mess this up. I'm fixing it. I only have to think back to her lying on the ground in fear of me after claiming her. That's enough to solidify my decision to keep pushing her. She will learn to trust me again. The fucked-up part is that I think she's really pissed that now I know she can be shaken. Like it somehow makes her weak. That's a load of shit. My mate is anything but weak.

The building is small and it's easy enough to encircle it, drawing in air as I go.

I pause as I scent the air, detecting a number of vampires in the tall grass by the fence. It's easy to catch the trail. I move to follow it through the field but stop short, thinking I shouldn't leave my mate for too long. It's only a moment for me, only seconds until she's back in my sight. I can smell her and feel her even. The thought of leaving her alone, though, even if only for a moment? I don't fucking like it. That tightness in my chest eases as I see my mate's fingers on her neck, running along the little indents of the scar I gave her.

Knowing she very much feels me as I do her, I stride to the passenger side and open the door for her.

"I'll drive," she demands as she walks to the driver's side, ignoring my attempt to reconcile.

Just as she opens the door, I tell her, "It would be better if I drive. After all, I'll be trying to scent our way." She purses her lips and clicks her tongue against the roof of her mouth before striding toward me, her heels tapping out a staccato rhythm on the pavement. "Fine, pup."

Before she can slip into the seat, I wrap my hand around her waist, holding her there. Tension crackles between us as her chest rises and falls. My gaze is locked with hers.

"I want us to be okay," I admit to her in a whisper. Her fingers wrap around mine, releasing my grip as she swallows and says, "Me too."

That's all I get. But it's better than nothing.

It's silent in the car as I pick out the way to go. Veronica's still and quiet.

There's an out-of-sync energy that surrounds us and I despise it. The atmosphere is so different between us. It's as though we're at war, but neither of us wants to be fighting. It takes less than half an hour until I find a gravel road. It reeks of vampires. Far more than what I smelled back at the donation center. Braking, I stop the car. I squint down the road, but it's too difficult to make out what it leads to.

I look to my mate and tell her, "We should continue from here on foot." Watching her hand open the door, suddenly I'm not liking that she's with me. I'm slow. They could outrun me, but they could also grab her. They could take her and do to her whatever the hell they're doing to the other vampires. And what could I do? If they stay to fight, I'll win. My strength is unmatched. But their speed is superior. They could easily outrun me. They could take my mate captive and leave me nothing but a trail to follow.

"Wait." My voice is far too loud, considering vampires are close. She leans into the car with her hands braced on the doorframe.

"What the hell, Vince," she hisses. "You need to be quieter."

"Get in the car." Her eyes narrow at me, not liking

my tone. "Baby, there are too many vamps. I don't trust it."

"We'll be fine, Vince."

"I won't be able to live with myself if something happens to you."

"I'll be fine; stop worrying. I can handle myself." She stresses the last part, shifting her stance and the gravel crunches beneath her heels.

"No, I can't live if something were to happen to you." Sadness flashes across her eyes and I don't understand it.

"You'll be just fine if I die. You'll have to learn to live with it." Her hard words seem out of place with the sorrow reflected in her dark eyes. It takes a moment for me to grasp what the hell's going on. My hand slams against the wheel in anger as it hits me. She's going to have to keep living after I die because she's a vampire, not a wolf. I'm such an insensitive asshole. She jolts at my harsh movement.

"I'm sorry. I wish things could be different." I barely get the words through my gritted teeth. I haven't really thought about the fact that my mate is immortal. What the hell is wrong with me? "Get in the car."

"I'll be fine, Vince."

"Get in the damn car right now, Veronica. I'm not going to risk losing you. I will *never* risk you." She fidgets outside the car, her feet gently moving the rocks beneath her again, and for a moment I think she's going to ignore me and walk down the path without me. Instead, she quietly gets in the car and shuts the door with a faint click, staring straight ahead while I gaze at her.

"You'll be fine if I die, Vince. You'll have to be fine and just keep living." Her head turns to face me and her cold dark eyes are devoid of emotion when she tells me, "You can't keep me by your side forever." Her words cut deep into me.

"I'll keep you safe for as long as I live, I promise you." I move to grasp her hand and she lets me. Even as the cords in her neck tighten with a swallow, she lets me hold her hand in mine. I brush my lips against her knuckles and turn her hand over to kiss her palm. "You're mine to keep by my side if I wish."

Her sigh is one that will stay with me. One of stubbornness, hardness, and a somber note of regret. It fucking kills me. She rests her hand in her lap while I start the car and leave the trail. I'll call Devin and tell him what we've discovered as soon as I swallow this lump climbing up my throat. There's no need for us to go down that path into God knows what by ourselves, most likely outnumbered. We're a pack for a reason.

"Do you want to talk about it?" I murmur the words while I drive us toward home. "We should make it there in a few hours. Plenty of time to talk." Before she can answer, my phone's timer goes off, indicating it's time to call Lev. I wait a moment and Veronica only shrugs, her gaze focused on the phone. Reluctantly, I put it on speaker and the other end rings once before Lev picks up.

"Yo, you good?"

Clearing my throat, I tell him, "Yeah, heading back now."

"No leads?" Lev's disappointment is obvious.

"We got something. We're going to need backup, though." I can practically feel his grin through the sounds of his howling laughter. My first thought is new to me: he doesn't have a mate to protect. There's not an ounce of worry for him. "We'll be back soon."

"Still, check in with me again in an hour. I don't need Devin up my ass."

"You got it." I end the conversation and glance at my mate. "Baby, talk to me."

"What do you want me to say?" she's quick to respond, but doesn't look back at me.

"Are we all right?" Her dark eyes find mine and I decide to pull over to have this conversation. There's a hint of worry laying heavy on my shoulders and I can't fucking stand it. Putting the car in park, I push the seat as far back as I can so I can pull my mate into my lap. She gasps as I lift her up and settle her right where I want her.

Both of her palms brace against my chest. Her eyes are wide and the vulnerability she tries to hide shines back at me. I'm gentle as I brush her hair back from her face with my knuckles. Her skin is smooth and that simple touch forces her to close her eyes.

"I need to know we're okay, baby. I know I pushed you. I was just trying to help and I'm worried I did the opposite of what I wanted."

"I know you were. It's fine." She shrugs off my concerns, the cords in her neck tensing as she swallows. My entire body bristles at how she tries to play it off. Her tone is glib, but her body language isn't.

"It's obviously not fine," I answer, my voice louder than I wish it was. She tenses but I don't stop, telling her, "You aren't the same. I'm sorry, baby." Taking her chin in my hand, I force her to look at me. "I love you and I'm sorry."

"I know, and I love you too. I do." Her words act

as a balm, easing the tension and numbing the burning concern that's had me twisted up all day long. Her hand rests on mine and she waits a moment before admitting, "I'm trying to be okay with being scared."

"You don't have anything to be scared of."

A soft smile that's far too sad pulls up her lips and she says, "I'm already scared of what I'm going to do when you're gone … and how that's going to feel."

"Baby," I breathe and my fingers spear through her hair. "Don't think about that."

All she does is huff and then her eyes drop to my lips. "I love you. You know that, don't you?"

My lips crash against hers instantly. Parting her lips with mine, I suckle her top lip. "I know," I groan. "I love you too." Her fangs gently graze my lips, making me moan into her mouth. She rocks her body against my hardening length.

"This. This is something I never dared to want or dream," she tells me as her back straightens and she spreads her legs wider.

My head is instantly cloudy with lust. Her lips drop to my neck and her fangs slip down my tender skin. I let my head fall back, giving her more room. "Don't tease me, baby. I need you so fucking bad."

"Aww, is my pup hurting?" A smile creeps onto my lips at her teasing. *That's my mate.*

"You know I am. I've been wanting inside you all damn day." She climbs off of me and my wolf growls at the loss of her touch, making my eyes instantly widen. I force my wolf to stay back, knowing she's not going to tease me. Not too much, at least.

She settles in her seat, making me think maybe she is just fucking with me. *Shit.* I can't take being teased like this. Not with this tension between us. Her hands slip up her skirt and she slides her lace panties down her slender, long legs. Over one heel and then the other until they're off. *Fuck yes.* My hands fly to my zipper so I can unleash my cock, precum already beading at my slit. I need to be inside of her as soon as fucking possible. I lift my ass up so I can pull down my jeans and stroke myself a few times, waiting for her to climb on top.

She gracefully straddles me more quickly than should be possible, and easily slides down my length before I can do anything to help her. *Fuck,* she's so damn wet and hot. And fucking tight. I moan as she pushes herself all the way onto my dick.

"Fuck, baby. You feel so fucking good." My hands rest on her hips and she stills for a moment. I close my eyes and hold my breath, hoping I haven't scared her off. I only dare to breathe again once she starts moving up and down, stroking my dick with her hot pussy. My hands remain on her hips and my fingertips dig into her flesh, but I don't dare take control. She'll give it to me when she's ready, but for now I'll be patient.

"You want me to let you go?" I offer and she only shakes her head, her eyes closed as she practically fucks herself on my cock.

I nip her neck. As I do, her dark nipples harden and I'm tempted to rip her clothes from her. To tear them off and take her how the beast inside me wants to.

It's what the beast inside me wants, but there's not an ounce of me that would dare. That would risk frightening or triggering her in the least. I tilt my hips up so the angle lets me fill her deeper, lets me hit the back of her cunt and her bottom lip drops down with the faintest mewl of pleasure. Giving her this is all I want.

"Tell me what to do, baby."

Her head falls forward to rest on my shoulder as her pace picks up and I have to let go of her to grab the wheel behind her. If my hands stay on her, I'm going to take control. I'm barely able to keep myself from bucking into her and pounding into that sweet heat of hers. The smell of her arousal and the little moans pouring from those dark red lips have me on edge. Sensing my growing need, Veronica stops and puts her hands on my shoulders.

"Take me, Vince." My eyes shoot to hers, finding her nothing but serious. "Take me again. I want you to claim me again."

I don't hesitate to take control. "Turn around." She quickly spins around and positions my cock at her hot entrance. Gripping her hips, I pound her wet hole as my heels dig into the floor of the car. I piston into her tight pussy and nip at her shoulder. She moans in pleasure at the feel of my teeth grazing her neck. I refuse to lose focus. I need to pay attention to her reaction and make sure I don't cross the line.

I concentrate on the sound of her soft whimpers as her pussy pulses around my dick with the need to come. My hand reaches around to her front and I rub ruthless circles against her clit. She writhes beautifully, the pleasure taking over. She throws her head back and it lands on my shoulder, exposing her neck to me and making it that much easier to put my teeth right where her claiming mark is. The time has passed to truly claim her, but I'll give her exactly what she wants. And at the next full moon, I'll sink my teeth into her neck and claim her as my mate once again.

It's not a normal thing, to claim a mate twice. But we both need this. And I'm sure as fuck not going to deny her. Her pussy spasms on my dick and nearly has me finding my release as I slam into her to the hilt, but my eyes are centered on her expression, making sure it's only pleasure that has her trembling in my arms.

"Vince," she says, moaning my name. I lick her neck and watch as her body jolts from my touch. It makes me smile. As aftershocks pulse through her body, I ease my still-hard dick out of her and push the head against her ass. Her eyes pop open at the foreign touch. "Vince." This time my name on her lips is a warning. I'm ready to push her a little. Now that she's sated and has more control than she did when she was chained, I think she'll give it to me.

Moving her arousal to her puckered hole, I press a finger in and then another, making sure there's enough to lubricate her.

"Grab the wheel, baby, and don't you dare let go." She hesitates to obey, but her delicate hands grip the wheel as I ease into her. Her sharp fangs sink into her bottom lip and the sight alone has me leaking more and more into her. I watch closely as inch by inch of my cock slowly disappears into her ass. *Fuck me.* I press in deeper and don't stop, burying myself to the hilt as she squirms on top of me.

"You are so fucking sexy, so damn strong and fierce," I tell her as I move in and out of her slowly. "And you know what I'm going to do with you? With my powerful mate?" I nip her earlobe as she moans in ecstasy. "I'm going to come in your ass."

Fuck, just saying the words almost has me losing it. Thrusting harder into her, I pick up my pace. Her arousal leaks out of her pussy, dripping between us and down my thighs. Veronica's moans match my groans and I kiss her neck frantically. My eyes don't leave her face, though.

I need to make sure she enjoys this. I'm going to push her and take from her, and make her fucking love it. I buck into her over and over again until I feel my balls tighten and lift, and that familiar tingle pricks at my spine. "I'm going to come in your tight ass and you better fucking come with me."

The rough pad of my thumb strokes her clit again and again, demanding another orgasm from her. My fangs dig into her neck; the move makes her body tremble as she screams out with another release. I dig my teeth further into her soft flesh as I pound into her ass four more times until I shoot wave after wave of cum into her. I don't let up on her clit or release her neck until I've drained every bit of her climax from her.

She lays limp in my arms as she comes down from the high. I smile in satisfaction, knowing I've taken her and she enjoyed me being in control. I lick away the bit of blood on her neck and kiss the new mark. A satisfied rumble barrels through my chest; my wolf is finally settling.

Nuzzling into the crook of her neck, I ask her, "Did you enjoy that, my mate?"

She softly murmurs, "I love you so much." Her heavy head drifts to the side as her lips find mine. Finally, I feel like everything is going to be all right. I nip her top lip, which makes her smile and my wolf howls with pride.

"Vince?"

"Yeah, baby?"

"I'm thirsty." Her dark eyes focus on my neck as she licks her lips. *Fuck, yeah.* My dick twitches, still inside her.

"Go ahead, baby," I tell her and arch my neck so she can dig in.

Her small laugh draws my attention back to her. "Can I take my hands off the wheel?" My smart-ass mate. I give her a kiss on her cheek.

"Yeah, baby, let go. I've got you."

PART III

Immortal Love

CHAPTER ELEVEN

Devin

"COME ON, SWEETHEART, DON'T LOOK AT me like that." I don't even recognize my own voice as I plead with my mate to be reasonable. Yet again.

"Like what?"

"Like you're pissed at me and ready to fight." Steam is still drifting from the bathroom door I just walked out of and I can tell she's ready to lay into me again. I fucking love her fire, but damn, what the hell did I do now?

"I don't want to fight and I'm not mad." Grace crosses her legs in the center of the bed and lowers her head. I watch as she bunches the covers around her naked waist and pulls at the threads on the comforter.

"Then why are you pouting?" I don't understand my mate and her emotions. Humans should come with a fucking handbook.

"I don't want you to go. I'm nervous something bad is going to happen." Her raw confession is laced with vulnerability as she looks up at me through her thick lashes. Her hazel eyes are brimming with un-warranted hope that I'll stay with her rather than head out to Still Waters.

Fuck.

Striding over to the bed, I run the towel over my face and hair once more before dropping it to the floor. The chill on my damp skin does nothing to calm my growing erection. Seeing her naked on a bed, how could I not be hard? Even if she is mad at me. Shit, her anger only fuels my fire. It only makes me want to tame her that much more.

"I won't be gone long." I pick her up easily and settle her ass in my lap where she fits just perfectly. She nestles her head into my chest and runs her fin-gers through that bit of hair above my belly button that trails down to something else I'd rather she play with. I shut down those thoughts and concentrate on my mate. I need to distract her and get her pre-occupied with something before I go. "Have you decided what you want to do?" She surprises me when she nods into my chest. She lifts her chin and meets my eyes for the first time since I came into the room.

"I want to start a charity with Lizzie. For abused children."

"Humans?"

"Yes, of course." *Of course.* I resist the urge to tell her no. I can give this to her. It'll be a pain in the ass and she'll fight me with all the restrictions I'll have to put on her, but if she really wants it, I'll bend over backward to give it to her.

I'm not sure what part she doesn't understand, but that life and her are over. Or at least they're supposed to be. Those are the laws set forth. If a human is taken, they are dead to that world. If not, then the well-protected secrets of our lives can bleed into the human realm. We can't allow that to happen.

"It will have to be done under a false name. Also, you won't be able to make public appearances or be seen at all."

She readjusts in my lap before going back to picking at nothing on the blanket. "But I'll be able to see what they do, right? And set up events and monitor how they help the kids?"

A million questions filter through my mind in response. I shut them down one by one, reminding myself that she'll learn. She'll be happy here one day. I should count myself lucky, after all. She has no family to crave to return to. Lizzie is here with her and she's adjusted quickly given she didn't know a damn thing about us prior to being taken.

With that in mind, I concede.

"You can do it the same way I run the banks. Have cameras everywhere. Hire a dedicated go-between who acts on your behalf and relays everything. You can be involved as little or as much as you'd like. I prefer being a silent partner. If you'd rather be more involved, then you can. You have to set up a business plan and a budget while we're gone. When I get back I'll set up a meeting with my consultant to get a time-line established. He'll prepare everything you need to get started." It'll be easy enough and if it makes her happy, then I'm happy to give her whatever it'll cost.

Her smile presses against my chest. She tilts her head to nuzzle her nose across the base of my throat with her eyes closed. She's so damn beautiful when she's content. I wish I could make her this happy all the time.

"I thought of something for you to do while I'm away."

She sighs sleepily and stretches, apparently ready to start the day now that she's gotten the green light for her charity with Lizzie. "What's that, *Alpha?*" My dick twitches at her use of the word Alpha.

I groan and lean my head back. "Say it again."

She smirks knowingly and says, "What's that?"

"Don't toy with me, Grace," I scold her smart ass. I'm even more determined to hear it on her lips as I realize it's the first time she's called me Alpha.

Heat races through me as she rises on her knees and straddles my thighs, bringing her eyes level with my mouth. She lifts that defiant little chin up and I swear to God if she picks a fight, I'm going to flip her ass over and fuck her into the mattress. She lets her voice come out soft and seductive when she says, "Me?" Her hand trails over my shoulders, sending a shiver through my body. I resist the urge to shudder as her nails gently run down my back. She keeps my gaze as she bites her lower lip before saying, "I would never toy with you." She parts her lips and I can practically feel the word begging to come out of her mouth. I wait with bated breath as she whispers the word, "Alpha."

My palms grip that lush ass of hers and I pull her lips to mine, my fingers digging into her flesh. I moan into her mouth, ready to push her down and rut into her. I've been taking it easy on her since the claiming, but she's healing nicely and isn't sore. Besides, she'll have a few days to recover while I'm gone and I want her to feel me every time she moves for as long as I'm gone. I smile against her lips and flip her ass over. She gasps, taking in a sudden breath as she lands on her hands and I steady her hips until her knees find purchase on the bed.

I don't miss how she smiles and that her thighs clench. She knows what's coming.

"That's my good girl."

I run my fingers through her heat, finding her slick and ready for me. I groan in satisfaction and my wolf claws at me to fuck her. As I prod her with my fingers to test her readiness to take me, she pulls away, catching me off guard.

My first thought is that I hurt her, but she's not red or swollen. "You okay?"

She turns her head, looking away and giving a short, muffled response. My forehead pinches in confusion as I bring my hands up in defense. A tic in my jaw pulses at my eagerness to be inside my mate. I must've missed something. My dick protests my hesitation. I put both of my hands back on her hips and ask, "Sweetheart, what's wrong?"

"I don't know." I still behind my mate. I just want to fuck her, but I hold back, knowing there's something off.

Grace rolls onto her back; I withstand the need to keep her where I want her and fuck away whatever thought is bothering her. I keep my expression straight as she looks up at me while on her back. My hands instantly go to the curve of her waist, my eyes traveling to her breasts.

"What don't you know, sweetheart?" Goosebumps appear on her body as I gently trail my fingers down her sensitive skin. She squirms under my touch.

"I don't know if I'm ready."

"Wait as long as you want to start it, my love. There's no rush and I'm sure Lizzie will understand."

"For a baby." I freeze at her confession. This is the one fight I've lost between us.

"I don't know if I'm ready." She picks at the blanket again and the loss of her eyes on me makes me want to rip the damn thing off the bed and rip it to fucking shreds. "Did you know Lizzie's pregnant?"

I grunt at the thought and tell her, "It's way too early to tell." Licking my lips, I bend down to take her nipple in my mouth. She doesn't protest. In fact, she runs her fingers through the back of my hair. Her nails gently scratch my scalp, urging me to do as I'd like. I pull away releasing my tight hold on her with a *pop*. Grace slaps my arm as I admire the bright pink mark on her breast.

"Dom and Caleb are convinced," she says. A low growl vibrates up my chest and out of my throat. I'm happy for them, if she really is pregnant, but I don't really give a shit about that right now. I'm far more concerned with the fact that my own mate is taking active steps to avoid getting pregnant. And she's currently avoiding getting fucked. Another low growl leaves me.

"I'm sure they both think the baby is theirs too." My head shakes of its own accord at their arrogance. "They can't know yet. It's too early to scent it."

Grace's face falls. "Oh. If she's not, she's going to be really upset."

"Don't worry about her, sweetheart. Her heat will come again and then Dom and Caleb will be fighting each other to be inside her." The more I think about it, the more I'm worried about her delivering pups. I don't think either of them will be truly content if they don't father the first pup. I keep my mouth shut, though. Grace tends to worry and intervene, and none of that is something she should be concerning herself with.

Running a hand down my face, I wish we were talking about us rather than them.

"She's so ready to be a mother. We've never talked about it, but she's sure she's ready." Her head falls to the side and she sighs while her eyes meet my gaze. "How can you know for sure that you're ready?"

I don't understand her question, either because I've always known I'd have pups or because all the blood in my body is currently pounding in my throbbing dick. "What do you need to be ready?" If she'll just tell me, I'll fucking give it to her.

"To feel ready. Once we have a baby, we can't go back and we've just met each other."

"What the fuck does just meeting each other have to do with anything?" A hint of my anger comes out in my words and Grace narrows her eyes at me.

"We haven't had time with just the two of us. If

I start popping out babies, then we really won't get any time for just the two of us."

"We'll have plenty of time while you're pregnant. Once the pups come, we'll hire help if you'd like time alone. That's an easy fix."

"I just don't *know* that I'm ready." I resist the urge to sigh in exasperation. She's fucking killing me here.

"It'll drive me crazy every heat, to know you're actively working against getting pregnant. Everything in me wants to breed you." My wolf howls in agreement. "Do you think you'll ever know that you're ready?" I pinch her chin between my forefinger and thumb, then ask her, "What are you afraid of?" Her hazel eyes widen at my question and she whips her head out of my grasp in anger.

"I'm not afraid! I just don't know." Her anger catches me off guard. We already covered this. I fucking caved already. I gave her what she wanted, but she's still fucking fighting with me.

"You told me that you weren't ready, so we're waiting. There's no reason to fight. Why are you yelling at me?"

"I'm not yelling!" She practically screams the words and I just stare back at her unreasonable ass.

After a moment, a heavy sigh leaves me and I

climb off the bed. My hard dick protests the movement, bobbing up and down with every movement. I rake my fingers through my hair.

"Where are you going?" she asks and I respond by grabbing her angry ass by the ankles, then dragging her to the edge of the bed.

"Nowhere, sweetheart." I flip her over and prop her ass up for me.

"Devin!" She scolds me but with my hand against her shoulders, her back bows perfectly. I half expect her to protest, to do anything other than close her eyes and moan.

"You worry too much," I tell her and then give her cunt a languid lick. "Right now I need you to do anything but that."

She writhes slightly, a sight to behold. The second I slip two of my fingers into her greedy pussy, she melts against my touch. Her back arches and she rests her head on the bed as I curve my fingers and stroke her sweet spot. I push my thumb against her clit without any mercy.

"You've got to come, sweetheart. You're too wound up." She moans something incoherent into the mattress and I smirk at the sight of my gorgeous mate letting her arousal get the best of her. She's not in heat anymore. This is just her, loving my touch and letting it soothe her.

I kiss the small of her back as her skin heats and she pulls slightly away from the sensation. Her pussy tightens on my fingers as a bit of her honey drips down my hand. Picking up my pace, I fuck her ruthlessly with my fingers. All her small whimpers fuel me and I can't help but think this is perfect. Pregnancy or not, we have time. So long as she's mine, it doesn't matter.

I lean my chest against her back and lick my mark before growling the command, "Give it to me," at the shell of her ear, letting the heat of my breath tickle her neck. She obeys like the perfect fucking mate she is and comes on my fingers. "Good girl."

Her body is still shaking with aftershocks as I thrust my dick in to the hilt. *Fucking perfect.* Her pulsing heat feels so damn good, trying to milk my cock. Her pussy knows exactly what she wants; at least I can satisfy part of her. Rocking into her slowly at first, I take my time enjoying the feel of her warmth. But I know my mate likes it rough.

I pull her closer to the edge and piston into her without any warning. She screams into the mattress as her little hands fist the blanket and her hips buck against mine. Her small body thrashes against my hold, but I don't let up. Instead I reach around her hips and start circling her throbbing clit.

"Fuck!" She lifts her head to scream and I know everyone in this damn estate is going to hear my mate come. And I fucking love it. Let them hear how I please her. How she submits to me. I slam into her wanting more of her cries of pleasure. My hips rock against hers as I pound into her tight sheath. My dick hits her cervix and I fucking love the feel of it.

She moans out my name as I push myself inside her deeper and hold it there. She claws at the sheets to get away from the pain of me stretching her and pushing her to her limit, but I know she fucking loves every second of it. "I want a baby." She barely says the words through her panted breaths.

My eyes widen at the admission. *Fuck!* Now that her heat's gone, now she wants a baby. I slam into her, punishing that sweet pussy as I lose myself in her. I'll fill her with my cum and do my damnedest to knock her up even though the odds are not at all in our favor.

As my cock pulses inside of her, I lean down and groan in the crook of her neck, "You want my cum? Your greedy pussy wants my cum, doesn't it?" I smack her ass so hard my palm stings and watch a red mark form on her flesh. I spank her ass again and again until she finally answers.

"Yes!" She moans out as another wave of arousal makes fucking her that much easier. Gripping her hips, I angle her to take the punishing fuck as deep as possible. I slam into her over and over again. Even as I feel her pulse around my dick and coat it with her cum, I don't stop.

I push deep into her as she thrashes on the bed beneath me. The sight and feel of her like this has my balls drawing up and a cold sweat breaks out over my skin. It takes four long, deep strokes to have her screaming in ecstasy. Her pussy tries to milk my cock and when I feel the tight walls squeeze and flutter around me, it's enough to set me off. I come hard and I stay deep inside her even when I know I'm spent. I pick her ass up and leave her like that.

"Don't move." I slip out of her only to get a cloth from the bathroom. My dick is at half-mast but when I come back to the room it springs to life at the sight of my mate, head down and ass up. Her hazel eyes watch me closely as I stride back to her. I smirk at my feisty mate, subdued from her orgasm. Her chest and cheeks are flushed, and her breathing is still ragged. "I prefer you much more when you're sated."

"Mmm." She murmurs a sound of agreement although I imagine she'll give me hell for it when she's more coherent. "I prefer you fucking me to telling me no," she manages. Her voice is coated in sarcasm but her smile is genuine. A deep, low chuckle rolls through me at her barely spoken words.

CHAPTER TWELVE

Dom

“**Y**OU STILL FEEL HER, BABY?”

My apprehensive mate nods her head with a weak smile playing at her lips. She's barely moved from the position she's in. She's so damn worried her wolf's going to leave her. It fucking kills me to see her like this, as a nervous wreck.

Sitting cross-legged in the field with the sun setting behind her, Lizzie looks just as apprehensive as she does wildly beautiful.

“Smile, baby. It's a good thing that she hasn't left.” Lizzie's hand rubs against her chest like she's petting her wolf. Like the kids at my old pack used to do. I chuckle at her. If it wasn't heartbreaking, she'd be adorable right now.

"Do you think she'll stay this time?" Her question is whispered, like she'll scare her wolf off if she speaks any louder. The half smirk on my lips vanishes when she peers up at me with tears brimming. My poor mate.

I shrug, trying to make light of the situation. I've noticed she mirrors what I'm feeling. If I'm serious, so is she; if I'm not, she's not either. "Sometimes my wolf goes on hiatus. It happens to all of us, and it's okay when it does."

"That's right, baby girl," Caleb says from behind me as he pulls his shirt over his head. He strips in the field, getting ready to shift. "My wolf loves going for a run, though." He smiles at our mate, eating up the distance between the two of them to help her up. It works. She stands easily enough although her hand stays on her chest. "He's especially excited that you're going to ride him, baby."

She smacks his arm and takes two small steps away from him before she says in a sultry voice, "Don't make it sound so dirty." He grabs her small hips and pulls her body into him to kiss his mark on her neck.

"You know you want to ride me." She blushes at his teasing words and I can't help loving that warmth of happiness that flows through me. I kick off my boots and watch the two of them. The sight of her smile makes me radiate with pride. We've come such a long way. I know she's always going to want her wolf to show herself. Being latent will only make it worse, but I'll do everything in my power to help her and her wolf.

"You want to get naked too, little one?" My dick hardens at the thought of our mate exposed and bared to us. "Your wolf may want to come out more if she feels the wind on your skin." I have no fucking clue if that's really true, but I don't mind telling a little fib so I can feel her bare pussy on my back. Caleb glances at me for a second like I'm a fucking liar and I don't give a shit. Then he smiles at my deviousness and plays along.

"Strip, baby girl." He gives her neck a hard open-mouthed kiss before releasing her. She bites her lip, but nods her head and starts undressing. I stroke my dick at the sight of her curves. Her full breasts bounce as she pulls the little dress over her head. There's a bit of a chill in the air, but the temperature's nice enough. She should enjoy the feel of the sun kissing her skin.

She bends over to put her clothes in a neat pile and I groan at the sight of her. My wolf wants me to push her down and take her. Caleb's palming his dick and I can see he wants the same thing. A low, possessive growl rips through me. The sound makes Lizzie jump a bit.

In the blink of an eye, Caleb shifts easily.

His black wolf trots to our mate and lowers his head. She's so small next to his beast. He licks her cheek, making her grin and she pushes his snout away letting out a peal of feminine laughter as she does. He whuffs and I shift as she spears her fingers through his thick fur.

The familiar crack of my bones is comforting and feels natural as I change form. My vision is heightened and my control waning but present. My wolf trots to her with ease and pride. He's a bit smug that he's larger than Caleb's wolf.

I shuffle back as Caleb lowers himself flat to the ground and she straddles him. My wolf whimpers with desire to see her wolf. He can smell her and he wants her more than anything. I huff at his impatience and rein him in. He may never get to see his mate, but at least he can smell her now.

Caleb takes off without warning, making Lizzie

cry out and then laugh as she clings to his fur. He heads straight to the forest and I know he must want to take her to the clearing where we claimed her. I round the bend and sprint, pushing my limbs and straining my muscles to get there first. I hurl my body over the boulders in my path and duck under a fallen tree. The wind rustles through my fur as my wolf strains and I push him to run faster. I hope she sees me. The bark of passing trees barely grazes my fur as I spring forward. I don't stop running even as my breathing quickens and my muscles tighten; I want her to see my wolf at his best. He huffs in agreement and leaps through the trees.

I slow my sprint as I round the bend and come to the clearing. Panting but proud. I trot toward the entrance and wait for them to come through the path. My wolf starts pacing and I give him control. He doesn't like that we let her out of our sight; he doesn't want to share our mate right now. I shake my body, ridding myself of the leaves and debris that cling to me from my run. I calm my breath and wait impatiently. After a moment I close my eyes and try to hear where they could be. I hear a laugh to my left and my wolf snorts at me, wasting no time to head to the stream. Damn, I thought he'd take her here.

"*You fucker.*" I hear Caleb laugh in my head at my words as I sprint to get to the stream. I'm faster in my wolf form so it doesn't take long to catch sight of them. My wolf growls low at the sight of Caleb pounding into Lizzie from behind. His fingers dig into her hips and each thrust makes her breasts bounce.

"*I couldn't help it,*" he groans out in my head as I shift and make my way toward them.

"*Selfish prick.*" He laughs at my admonishment.

"*Admit it, you would've done the same thing.*" I nod at his words as he continues thrusting into her. Lizzie moans in pleasure as her knees scrape against the ground and her palms dig into the dirt. Her long blond hair flows over her shoulder as she takes every one of Caleb's thrusts. Her head arches back with her eyes closed and her full lips parted while she whimpers for more.

Walking confidently up to my mate, I put my hand on her throat and drag it up to her chin. Her soft blue eyes slowly open and stare right into mine. She peeks at my erection and then looks back up to meet my gaze. Her mouth is agape with pleasure while Caleb continues thrusting into her. I stroke my dick a few times, watching how her body jolts with each of his powerful strokes. The remnant of a faint bruise on her neck can be made out and part of me wishes Caleb would go easy on her, knowing her pussy must be aching still too. But her loud moans and her body pushing back against his hips, keep my mouth shut.

I slip the tip of my cock between her lips and she shifts forward to take more of me into her mouth. My head falls back and I let out a groan as her warm mouth sucks down my dick. Her tongue massages the underside and makes me leak down her throat. She moans as I pulse in her mouth and the vibrations make my legs tremble with the heated anticipation and need to release. I gather her long hair in my hands and wrap it around my wrist. Gripping the hair at the nape of her head, I push myself into her mouth until I feel her throat give and constrict around my length. Fuck, she feels so fucking good. I pull out and give her a moment to catch her breath before sliding my dick to the back of her throat again.

Out of fucking nowhere, Caleb's fist comes down on my arm, making me drop my hand from her hair. She whimpers from the slight pain and I shoot fuck-ing daggers at Caleb. My wolf rears back and snarls at him.

"I can't fucking see when you do that." He doesn't slow his rhythm as he voices his concern in my head. It takes me a moment to register his words as Lizzie diligently takes my dick back into her mouth, oblivious to the fact that I'm two seconds away from ripping her other mate's head off.

"What?" My wolf snarls again, not liking that my attention is being pulled away from our mate's touch.

He shoves himself deep into Lizzie and holds her there, making her moan around my dick and try to push away from the intensity of his shallow movement.

"Don't fucking think of coming in her. I'm up next." I pull my dick out of Lizzie's mouth and push it back in slowly as he withdraws and strokes himself, aiming his dick at the small of her back. With his right hand wrapped tightly around his dick, his left moves between her legs making her writhe beneath him.

"Hold still, baby girl." He watches as I fuck her mouth, just waiting for the chance to get into her pussy.

"Switch with me." I hear his voice in my head, but I don't register his meaning until he's pushing me out of his way to shove his dick into her mouth. My anger is barely contained. *"You better come in her pussy. If*

not, I'm going again." I'm tired of him being in my head when all I want to do is give and take pleasure from our mate.

I grunt at him as I push my length into her heat. "Fuck, you feel so good." I start out nice and slow and within seconds she pushes against me, wanting more. I can't deny my mate. I rut into her with a primal need. I don't even realize Caleb's found his release until he commands her, "Swallow every drop."

I glance up from where my dick's ruthlessly pounding into her pussy to see her lick her lips and shudder with her impending orgasm. Caleb reaches down and pinches her nipples while biting her throat. She arches her neck and the sight of my mark on her has me coming in waves in her pussy. I reach around and pinch her clit to make sure she gets off and she does. *Holy fuck.* Waves of heat crash through me and make me dig my heels into the dirt. Pushing myself deeper into her, I wait for the aftershocks we're both feeling to subside before pulling out.

When I finally catch my breath and open my eyes, I see Caleb squatting in front of our mate, kissing her and nibbling her lip. She's still panting and struggling to stay up on all fours. Her skin's flushed and her legs are still quivering from the intensity of her release.

I take her small body in my arms and roll us to the ground, cradling her with her back to my chest. I lift her body on top of mine and run my hands over her trembling limbs, comforting her as best as I can.

"Don't be selfish." I ignore Caleb's scolding. I just want to fucking hold my mate.

"You had her first and I didn't give you shit about it, did I?"

"I didn't get to come in her. I count that as you giving me shit."

"Stop it!" Lizzie shouts and lifts her head from my chest to glare at the two of us. I blink at her pissed-off expression.

"How the fuck did she hear us?"

"Lizzie, can you hear us, little one?" I question her telepathically and wait for her response. I get nothing, not a damn thing.

"I'm sorry, baby girl." The fuckface decides he's going to scoop her off my chest to cuddle her and I grit my teeth to keep Lizzie from sensing how pissed I am. I don't want her getting upset again.

"Knock it the fuck off, asshole." I fucking hate that he's taking her from me. I only just lay down with her.

"You knock it off! You can keep petting her, but I get to hold her now."

"I told you two to stop it!" Lizzie pushes off of Caleb and makes to stand with her back toward us.

"You can hear us?" I'm overwhelmed with happiness, but as I search for her wolf, I can't feel her or hear her.

"Talk to us." Caleb pleads with her in my head, but she doesn't respond. Instead her shoulders start shaking and that gets both of us up on our feet.

"Don't cry, little one. We won't fight. I promise." I still don't know how the fuck she knew we were fighting. Rubbing her shoulders I try to console her, but she only sobs harder.

"You can't hear me!"

Caleb looks to me before answering her, "We heard you, baby. We'll stop fighting. Dom's just a little moody today."

"No, you can't hear me! I keep talking to you. I can hear you, but you can't hear me." Her voice cracks and the realization breaks my fucking heart.

"Your wolf can hear us?" My wolf paces inside of me at the mention of his mate.

Lizzie nods and buries her head into Caleb's chest while reaching for my hand. I take her little hand in mine and squeeze it while gently rubbing her back.

"Try again." My softly spoken words are meant

to offer her comfort, but her head rears back and she practically spits at me.

"I am! I'm screaming in my head and you can't hear me!" Tears spill down her reddened cheeks as she shudders from the chill of the air.

"Let's go home," Caleb speaks into Lizzie's hair, but he glances at me with a pained look. I'm sure I share his expression. We don't know how to help our mate. I don't like feeling helpless but that's exactly the situation I'm in right now.

"It's all right, little one. She isn't ready for us to hear her, that's all."

"We'll keep on loving you and one day she'll learn to trust us and let us in."

"You can't know that," Lizzie says. Her words are hard, but then she softens her tone to add, "What if she never does?" She sobs into Caleb's chest. My poor mate.

Caleb pulls away so she has to look at him when he answers, "Then she never does and life will go on. Everything will still be perfect. It might even be a good thing. When we have pups, you'll be able to listen in and they won't hear you."

I chuckle at Caleb's reasoning and add, "Our pups won't be able to get away with shit." Lizzie looks between the two of us as a small smile plays at her lips.

"You two won't be able to get away with anything either." She wipes under her eyes and rubs her hands against her thighs, pulling herself together. "I really don't like it when you fight."

"I'm sorry, baby, I was just fucking with Dom. I'll stop." Fucking Caleb, why's he gotta be the hero?

"I'll stop too. I don't want you to get upset." She cuddles into my chest and I kiss her hair. Her warmth and touch are everything. I can't imagine hearing but not being heard. My poor mate.

"I love you two," she whispers and molds her body to mine. Caleb and I both murmur our love for her and as unfortunate as it is, there's a bond that's unbreakable. It's stronger with every small step. Forward or backward.

"Time to go home, baby. They'll be heading out soon and I'm sure Grace is going to be lonely with Devin leaving her behind. You want to ride one of us, or do you just want to walk?" Caleb runs his hand up and down her back while he talks and I can tell she's losing her energy.

"My feet are going to hurt if we walk."

"Piggyback ride?" he suggests. A grin covers his face and I snort a laugh at his words.

Her head turns to face Caleb and she smiles as she says, "You're going to make such a good father." She leans away from him and gives me a kiss on the lips before looking into my eyes. "You too, Dom. You're going to make a great dad too." My chest fills with a sense of pride that spreads warmth through my entire body. "I got to ride you up here, so I'll ride Dom back." She pats Caleb's chest and gives him a quick kiss on the lips.

"We're going to be just fine, little one." I say the words in my head and she meets my eyes, acknowledging that she heard me. I reward her with a quick kiss.

"We love you, baby." Caleb kisses his mark before he shifts. I follow his lead and shift in front of our mate. She runs her hands through my hair before settling on top of me and gripping onto my fur.

"I love you too. Both of you."

CHAPTER THIRTEEN

With my car parked behind Vince and Veronica, I kill the ignition. The rumble fades as he does the same and all that's left is the quiet, dark night.

Neither of us gets out just yet … there's a third party we're waiting on. I check the clock and he should be here soon. It only took a few hours to get here, but I'm already missing my mate. Lev was pissed he had to stay behind, but I wanted him and the Betas to keep our human mates safe.

Vince is attached to the coven and I'm Alpha; this task falls squarely on our shoulders.

I glance in the rearview to see Alec park behind me. There's a man seated on the passenger side I don't recognize. I've never met him before and I'm not sure I like the fact that he's here. A heads-up would have been nice. It takes me a second to register that he's a vampire and there's another vamp in the back of Alec's car. I'm not sure why Alec thinks he can trust them and I'm real fucking reluctant to let my guard down.

This surprise isn't something I would ever expect from Alec. Bristling and already irritated, I message Vince that it's time.

I shut the door as quietly as I can and wait for him to walk with me to the edge of the gravel path. It'd be far too noisy to drive up the path. It would give our arrival away as well. They'd have plenty of time to bolt, so we'll be taking it by foot.

Veronica leans against their car, eyeing the fuck out of the two vampires Alec brought. She isn't subtle and I'm guessing she's not too keen on the fact they're here either.

"How many do you think?" I question Vince.

"No clue." He takes a whiff of the air and adds, "It's stronger than yesterday."

"Just the three of you?" Alec's steps are so quiet I didn't notice he'd come up behind me. I don't give that shit away, though. I continue looking down the gravel road and nod before turning to face him.

"I didn't want our mates to be left alone."

Alec nods and says, "Makes sense." He takes a deep breath and motions the two vampires to come over to us.

"I want to introduce you to my allies, Devin." He stares hard at me while he speaks. *Allies?* My spine stiffens and my wolf raises his hackles. I suppress his growl. These are not friends. Alec's lip rises in an asymmetrical grin as my stern response registers with him that I've understood his meaning.

"They're enemies, Vince." I speak the words calmly to Vince so he can pick up what Alec has insinuated. The fact that Alec confirmed my gut feeling heightens the anticipation for a fight. Vince makes no outward sign that he's heard me, but I can feel his anger and readiness to rip them apart. He calls Veronica over and wraps a possessive arm around her before murmuring something in her ear. I can't hear what it is, but the two vampires huff humorously with thinly veiled judgement at Vince's display of affection.

My eyes stay on Veronica, watching her as she takes in the knowledge Vince is giving her. She narrows her eyes at Vince and takes in a heavy inhale before nodding in understanding. He responds with a kiss in her hair.

"Nice to meet you two," I begin and wait for Alec to give me any more clues or signals. The plan was easy enough before, but this adds a speed bump I wasn't expecting and now I second-guess if the plans we had are realistic at all. Has our cover been blown and this is nothing more than a setup? We could be walking into a giant trap for all I know.

"This is Marcus and Theo," Alec says, pointing to his left and then right. The vampires nod respectively. "Meet Devin, the Alpha of the Shadows Fall pack. This is Vince, and his mate."

"So you're the vampire who aligned with the werewolves?" Vampire Prick Number One speaks over Alec to Veronica. "I didn't realize wolves even mated vampires."

Vince appears calm and easygoing on the outside, like he always does, but I know inwardly he's fuming. He looks to his mate with a smirk and rubs her back. She leans into his embrace before engaging with the vampire who spoke. "It's rare. I got lucky, I guess," she tells him. One of the two snorts at her response and her calm smile turns to ice.

"She's going to fuck them up. I can feel it." Vince

smiles at his mate like everything's fine while his irate voice echoes in my head.

"Did you tell her what's going on?"

"Can't. They would hear. But she'll pick it up fast."

"Devin, your guns are in the trunk. Marcus and Theo, I brought guns for you too." Alec pops his trunk with a click of his key fob and the vampires and I head to the car trailing behind him. I have no fucking clue what guns he's talking about, but I'm happy to accept whatever gifts he's decided to lend me. Adrenaline courses through me, every muscle tense as I round the car on high alert. I grin at the sight, not at all disappointed.

There are three semiautomatic pistols and an assault rifle.

"Fuck yeah." Vince's voice booms with excitement. "The rifle's mine, right, Alpha?"

I see Alec nod from the corner of my eye as he hands two of the pistols to Marcus and Theo, then stuffs the third into a holster at his hip.

"I don't think so, Vince." I pull the strap over my body and secure the weapon.

"Careful. It's all silver," Alec says.

"Silver?" Theo looks to Alec for confirmation while examining the bullets.

"I took the liberty of preloading everything." He meets the vampires' curious expressions and adds, "Aim to wound, but if you have to, killing is acceptable." The vampires exchange a glance, then nod and mutter that they understand, seemingly content with the orders.

"What's the plan?" I speak aloud, waiting for more direction and any information Alec can give me.

"Friends will be on the left," he says and turns to face the vampires. "That's where the exit is, correct?"

"No, the exit is on the right side. They're coming through there," one of them replies although neither look at him. The vampires are still examining the bullets rather than giving us their full attention. *Friends on the left.*

"Ah, got it." He looks me in the eyes and there's a beat that's serious and prolonged before he tells me, The Authority will get them from the right."

"*Vince, you got that?*" I start a silent dialogue with him.

"*Yeah, stay to the left. Is it just the vamps we're ambushing?*"

"*No idea. You sure you want to bring Veronica in on this?*"

"*They fucked with her coven. There's no way she's not getting in on the action.*"

"*You have to keep her safe.*" I know he already knows, but I can't help giving the command regardless. My mate is human, but even if Grace wasn't as vulnerable as she is, even if she was a vampire like Veronica, I still wouldn't want her here.

"*I told her to stay with me. She'll listen.*" I hope Vince's right.

"You expect them to be waiting for us?" Marcus asks Alec.

"Absolutely." He doesn't hesitate to answer. "If they're still monitoring the blood banks, they know we're onto them. If they planted a spy in the system, they know. I think it's fair to assume they know we're coming for them. They may already know we're here now."

"So we're walking into an ambush?" I question as though I have no idea what Alec is really orchestrating.

"We're going to ambush the ambush." His silver eyes flicker with anger, but he keeps it contained and flashes a wide smile, radiating a false sense of trust and calm.

My blood heats as I draw in a single deep breath.

There won't be time for hesitation. Masses have been slaughtered in seconds. We'll be in and it will be over in minutes at most.

Gripping the handle of the gun, I nod. "After you," I say and motion for Alec to lead the way, the two vampires following close behind him.

I'm locked and loaded and ready to get this shit over and done with so I can get back to Grace. My pulse races as we stalk down the grass that surrounds the gravel road. Each step quiet and in line with that of the others. I'd be quieter in wolf form, nearly silent as the vampires are now, but that would render my gun useless. And surely Alec gave it to me for a specific purpose.

Veronica hisses to reprimand her mate as Vince steps on a twig, breaking it and disrupting the quiet trail to our target. I doubt the vampires can hear us this far out, but it's best to keep perfect form until we're there.

I'm not sure if this is going to be a bloodbath, or if Alec has a plan to capture the vampires and force them to face a trial. With every silent step, my heart races faster, prepared for what may come. It's slow and steady, and every second tense and wound tight. We're only about halfway there when a loud bang shocks the quiet night. It came from the warehouse a mile or two in front of us.

The vampires take off almost too fast to register, forming a blur in front of us. I push my limbs as fast as they can go, but it doesn't even come close in comparison. Veronica's form rushes past me and the gust of wind from her speed comes a second later.

"Stop." Vince forces the word out as he gains momentum and nearly passes me. Veronica halts just outside the stairs to the warehouse. She's fuming with rage and her chest is frantically heaving in air as her fists shake at her sides. Her dark eyes follow us as we get closer to her.

"Stay behind me." Veronica doesn't respond aloud to Vince's command, but she doesn't go in without him either.

The tension between those two is thick. It's an unwanted distraction at this moment. If they can't do this, if my attention is spent on the two of them being safe, this could all go to shit.

"I've got her," he reassures me and I keep moving, passing her, following Alec as he sprints toward the double doors. All I can do is trust that he's right, that she'll catch on and that she'll listen to him.

As I rush to come up behind Alec, keeping to

his left, he lifts his hands and gestures in the air. The doors are torn off their hinges and crash hard on the cement as he nears them. It's eerily quiet. Not at all what I expected. There's a noticeable lack of gunshots or screaming. *Nothing.* I don't trust it. My heart hammers in my chest. I slow my pace, planting one foot in front of the other and stand to the right of the opening as Vince and Veronica come up from behind me.

"I'll go in first, follow behind. Don't get blocked in, Vince. If I go down, run. Don't look back."

"Fuck off, Dev. That shit's not happening." I growl at his response, but quietly make my way through the doors. I sweep the room, aiming my gun to the right and left, quickly taking in my surroundings.

There are too many people in this space for me to feel anything close to comfortable. On the left half of the room are two witches, both female and both with pissed-off expressions and clearly irritated. I don't recognize either of them, but their green eyes and wild red hair suggest they're related.

In the center of the room are three humans bound and gagged, tied to chairs with silver rope. The acrid smell of their urine makes me cringe as they audibly struggle, their eyes wide with fear.

I walk in a slow line across the room, keeping

my left shoulder pointed at the witches and my gun trained on the center of the room. Alec stands before the humans, but his eyes are on the eleven vampires off to the right. Behind them are two more sorcerers and a shifter, that fucker, Remy. Carol is also among them. If my math's right, that makes eleven vampires and one shifter against three sorcerers, three witches, and the three of us. The numbers aren't in our favor. But with our strength and the magic on our side, we should come out the victors, with little to no casualties. If they're smart, they'll surrender. But then again, if they were smart, they wouldn't have crossed Alec.

Natalia stands in front of Alec, waiting for him to speak. She appears confident and strong before him, but the miasma of fear surrounds her. "We got here just before you. Luckily they were easy to round up."

"Humans?" His question is laced with disbelief.

"We found two dead vampires in a silver cage in the back." She gestures at them, then faces Alec and stares into his eyes as she faintly laughs. "These humans tried to outrun us."

Heat engulfs me as the tension swells.

"Humans!" The room shakes with his anger as he roars the word. The witches to my left spread their arms wide as thunder explodes above us; the doors and windows of the warehouse suddenly close in on themselves, crumpling the steel and brick in an unnatural way, caging all of us in and cutting out all light save for the three large dome lights above us.

Fuck. My pulse hammers and I stay steady, prepared but on edge. Waiting and praying I don't react too slowly.

Natalia shudders at the witches' display of power. The vampires behind her shift slightly on their feet. Marcus and Theo slip their pointer fingers onto the trigger of the guns Alec gave them. They may be fast, but with nowhere to run, their speed will be irrelevant. Adrenaline spikes through me. A sweat breaks out along my skin and I welcome it. I crave to let my beast out, but I wait. Alec will give me a sign when it's time. My body begs to shift, I remember the gun and fight the need to shift even harder.

"Stay behind me." I hear Vince's command come from my right, but my eyes stay forward, focused on the scene in front of me.

"You thought I'd fall for this?" Alec sneers at Natalia.

"Fall for what? You think I'd betray you?" Her eyes flash with anxiety, but her voice is level.

"I know you would." Alec speaks his words slowly

as Natalia's anger gets the best of her. Waves of fear drift from the line of vampires. I watch Remy as he slowly retreats from the crowd. He has no escape now that the witches have closed everything off.

Natalia's shoulders rise and fall as she slowly backs away from Alec. Her gaze stays glued to him as she nears the line of vampires behind her. She's a caged animal with wild, desperate eyes. The realization that she's trapped and Alec knows what she's done hits both her and the rogue vampires in unison.

I steady my breathing and concentrate on the location of each vampire. Remy is the only other enemy to watch for. But he'll be slow enough to see coming. Just as I clench my fist, all hell breaks loose. The quiet is shattered with shrieks of pain and growls of rage.

I'm not sure who to take down first, but as I block a vicious attack from one vampire, I witness Theo and Marcus aim their guns at Alec and pull the trigger. In a split second, everything seems to slow. A shock of white shoots through both Theo and Marcus, forcing them to the ground as their bodies shake uncontrollably. Their limbs continue to twitch, rendering them useless.

Gritting my teeth, I keep an internal count. Two down, ten to go. Alec was smart enough to level the

playing field immediately by sabotaging their weap-
ons. I growl in triumph that we were the first to take
the numbers down.

The vampires spread out in a blur behind them
and attack in pairs. The two sorcerers and Carol are
instantly surrounded. A beam of blue sends two vampires flying in the air and slamming against the wall
behind me; it won't kill them, but at least it gives us
time to get to the other side.

With every muscle wound tight, I run forward
trying to reach Carol as two vampires attack her in
unison. One behind her and one in front. Both of
them bite into her neck and pin her to the ground.
Witches have power, but their strength and speed
are poor. She's knocked down to the ground as they
drain her of her blood, weakening her. As soon as I
reach her petite body, I jerk the nearest vampire off
of her. His fangs rip her flesh, spraying blood in front
of me as I grab his chin in my right hand and hold
his body still with my left arm. He frantically pulls
against me, trying to gain freedom, but I strain my
muscles against his struggle and twist his neck, shat-
tering his spine. His bones crack and I drop his limp
body, knowing that's another one gone.

I lunge for the other vampire, prepared to fight

him off of Carol, but he's convulsing on the ground with blood that's nearly black spewing from his mouth. My eyes find Carol on the ground, barely moving. Her wounds are seeping and I bend to cover them with my hand and stop the flow until she can heal herself. She coughs blood from her cherry lips and smiles at me.

"Silver doesn't hurt us, even in our blood." Her eyes twinkle with trickery as she pushes my hands away. They're soaked with her blood and I realize she knew about Alec's plan. Who else knew?

Adopting a protective stance over her weak body, I take in what remains of the chaos as she hums and slowly heals her wounds. It's taking far too long, but I can't leave her alone and vulnerable. I stand guard and scan the room, searching out Vince and Veronica. Veronica's going head to head with Natalia, and Vince is fighting off Remy. He's not fully committed to this battle, his gaze darting to his mate with distress far too often. A snarl rips up my throat from my chest. Alec is fighting off two vampires at once, and the other two sorcerers and two witches are facing off with a vampire each. We're on the verge of losing this battle. My blood heats and pumps through me, urging me to fight.

A roar leaves me as I allow the anger to take over. The pure rage and animosity. The need to return to my mate and end this battle just as quickly as it began.

Carol slowly rises to her feet. She's still weak and in no condition to be left alone, though. If a vampire attacks her, she won't make it. Even so, I can't just stand back and watch them die; Alec is being slashed repeatedly as the vampires break through his defense and get in small hits each time. Blood sprays from his wounds as knives slit his flesh.

"Go." Her weakly spoken word is all I need to run to Alec. I push my back against his, giving him support as I wait for the inevitable blows. With our backs protected, the vampires can only attack us head-on, giving us a better chance at defending ourselves. In a blink, a gash is slashed across my face. Another blur and a gush of wind whip in front of my face. My arm reaches in front of me, but I catch nothing. The fucker is too fast. My wolf roars in anger.

Thump, thump, my blood pounds.

"Your gun!" Alec reminds me of the weapon strapped to my body. My fingers reach for the trigger at the same time that the vampire attacking me tears it from my body. The instant the trigger is pulled, there's a loud bang and a blinding flash of white. Instinctively

I reach up to shield my eyes from the bright light. As I drop my hand and open my eyes, I gaze in wonder. Everything has slowed before me. The once loud surroundings are now a haze of white noise.

The gun is slowly being turned to face me as the pale vampire points it in my direction. I'm able to easily snatch the gun from the vampire's grasp and smash it across his face as his body seemingly continues to defy time and gravity.

Cold drifts around me as I move, seamlessly and easily while others are trapped for only a moment in this warped field.

I watch in awe as time speeds once again and the sound of screams ring in my ears, seeming louder than before. The vampire crashes on the ground and time returns to normal. My finger pulls the trigger and I welcome the flash of white as I barrel toward the still vampire and rip his throat out with my fangs. The magic relents quicker than before and time ceases to still for me as I watch Alec take the strike of a blade across his throat. I pull the trigger a third time and don't wait for the flash of light. I ram my body into the vampire, whose fangs are bared, prepared to feast on Alec's weakened body. I smash his head into the cement floor over and over without mercy. Even as time resumes, I continue bashing him into the hard, unforgiving ground until his skull breaks and his struggle becomes nothing.

Alec's body falls to the ground and he reaches for his throat. I crawl on the floor to reach him, but his eyes find mine before darting behind me in warning. I turn prepared for an attack, adrenaline spiking through my veins, but instead I see both Veronica and Vince losing their respective battles. Fear crushes down on me. Natalia and Veronica are each armed with blades, and they both have several pierced into their bodies. Veronica is much worse off, though, with a glaring gash down the front of her chest. Her body heaves, but her eyes are focused on vengeance.

Vince is struggling beneath Remy, both with their fangs out and snarling as they attempt to reach each other's throats. I quickly pull the trigger waiting for time to stop, for the moment to easily rip Remy into two, but time no longer obeys. I pull the trigger over and over as I run toward the two werewolves, wrapped around each other in a fight to the death. I toss the gun aside in a fit of anger as the magic no longer grants me an advantage and barrel into Remy's body, forcing him off of Vince. The second I have him pinned under me, Vince rises and quickly wraps his hands around Remy's throat, pulling with all his weight. I push my body on top of Remy's and wrench against Vince's strength. Remy screams in terror and pain as his neck snaps from the strain and his body goes limp.

I rise quickly, preparing for more, only to find myself surrounded by bloodshed. Carol hovers over Alec. Two sorcerers are surrounding the witches with white light. The vampires all lay dead, scattered in pieces across the large room.

The only noise is a violent hiss as Natalia and Veronica circle each other in the center of the room. Their dark, distorted dance of death has them weaving in and out among the humans who are still tied to the chairs, which have toppled over. Vince races to the center of the room, ready to help his mate.

"Behind me!" The bellowed command and the blur of Veronica's vision comes to form, her back to his. Natalia's body whips in front of Veronica's as Vince bends forward and Veronica leans her back against his as she wraps her legs around Natalia's neck, forcing the vampire to claw and slash at her legs. Vince moves as fast as he can, pushing the two vampires to the ground before grabbing Natalia's arms and pinning them behind her back. Veronica's legs bear several wounds. A deep gash in her upper thigh seeps blood as she squeezes her thighs around Natalia's neck, cutting off her oxygen.

Natalia struggles violently as she's forcefully contained between the two members of my pack. Veronica reaches forward and grips both sides of Natalia's mouth as she screams; she pulls with all her force against the vampire's jaws until they finally snap and separate. A shattered scream ricochets against the hard walls as Natalia's life is ended.

Vince releases the dead vampire, but Veronica's dark eyes are fixated on Natalia's tormented face. Her body is covered in blood and still badly wounded, but she disregards Vince as he tries to take her in his arms. Her fingers wrap around one of Natalia's fangs and she rips out the pair in turn before smiling in triumph at her dreadful victory. Vince raises his brows in question at his mate when she finally looks at him.

"For my queen." Her softly spoken words offer an explanation that Vince accepts as she heaves in a steadying breath. He opens his arms to her and she immediately goes to him, finally resting in his embrace.

They're safe. My pack is safe. Even that

knowledge doesn't grant me reprieve, though. I need my mate. With my shoulders heaving as I attempt to calm, all I know is that I need my mate.

"I'm glad they used the guns I gave them." Alec's voice resonates in the quiet warehouse as he walks slowly to where Theo's and Marcus's bodies lay, still trembling in shock. "They'll talk if they want to live. All we need is one to tell us what we want to know."

"Is it over?" I question, eager to leave and return to Grace.

Alec glances around the room before settling his kind eyes on me. His large hand raises and slaps against my shoulder.

"It's never over, my dear friend. But this battle has come to an end." He gives me a weak smile before walking to join Carol. No one has escaped unscathed, but we'll all heal. Except for the vampires who dared to betray the Authority. Two will live to give answers, but they won't live long after.

I will get back to my mate. I will love her and she will love me.

Heaving in a breath, I know that's all that matters. With death surrounding us and corruption in every corner of our world, our pack is safe and that's all that matters.

Grace

Devin hasn't taken his hands off of me. A warmth swept over me the second he stepped foot on the estate, and it hasn't left. With every soft hum that vibrates up his strong chest, it only intensifies. It's not the heat, it's something else that sparks between us. With his back braced against the threshold to the kitchen, he holds me close to him, his hand running soothing strokes up and down my back. His chin rests on the top of my head and every so often, he kisses my crown.

Each time he does, a smile is pulled to my lips.

Even if he was broken and bruised when he arrived, the shower seems to have cleansed all of that away. For each of them, every member of my pack.

The night has set and the sun will no doubt be rising soon, but the adrenaline hasn't left the room.

I shift against Devin to peek at Veronica and Vince in the corner nook of the room. Something's changed between them, something possessive and raw. Something that's dropped her guard and that's not the only noticeable change between them but it's so hard to place what's changed.

"Did something happen?" I whisper the question to Devin, peeking up at him through my thick lashes, exhaustion beginning to weigh my eyes down.

"Nothing that didn't have to happen. It all happened as it should." He kisses my temple and the warmth spreads throughout me once again as I close my eyes, feeling a familiar comfort I associate solely with my mate wash over me. "Fate conspired in our favor."

I can't help but whisper back, "Something's changed," and when I open my eyes, Veronica's sharp gaze meets mine. There's only a knowing look that she gives me before Vince cups her chin in his large hand and kisses her. He takes her lips with his and the gentleness between them is genuine and it shouldn't surprise me so, but it does. It's not unlike Caleb, Dom and Lizzie.

"A lot has changed very quickly, sweetheart," Devin murmurs into my hair and I shake my head, refusing to let the shift go.

"Something … something in the air is different," I say and the moment the thought leaves me, a chill runs down my shoulders. Devin's hand soothes the goosebumps that appear on my arm, running down my arm in the chill's wake.

In only his shirt and a baggy pair of gray sweats, I know I don't look glamourous, but I wanted to smell him. I wanted to feel him here when he was away. It helped, but not much. The lonesomeness that came over me … Lizzie felt it too. As if she heard her name in my thoughts, she glances over to me with a gentle simper. But my friend doesn't give me too much attention for too long. How could she, with both beasts on either side of her? Just as Devin hasn't stopped touching me, they haven't stopped touching Lizzie. The atmosphere is far more joyous between them, and I do feel the same relief, the same contentedness. I can't deny I feel whole in his arms.

I thought it would go away, though, this uncanny sensation, when Devin and the pack came back an hour ago, but it didn't. I repeat, more sternly, "Something's changed."

"The new moon is coming," Devin responds as if it's an obvious answer.

"What does that mean?"

"It just brings a different energy, different powers."

"Powers?" I question and he only smiles down at me, his dark and hungry gaze flashing with desire.

Sucking in a breath, I try to steady my racing heart as he tucks a lock of hair behind my ear.

"You have so much to learn, Grace."

That I can't deny.

I can't help but feel like this is only the end of a chapter for a story that hasn't finished yet. It's an eerie feeling that washes over me, and one that's only dimmed when Devin kisses me.

"I love you," Devin whispers at the shell of my ear and the warmth of his breath against the crook of my neck does more to me than any other feeling could. When he holds me like this and kisses me, it's as if the entire world can wait. It could stop, it could vanish, and I wouldn't even notice.

"I love you too," I whisper, my eyes closed as he takes my lips with his and deepens it.

Chapter Fourteen

Vince

Three days later

I KNOW SOMETHING'S OFF AS I WALK TO OUR room. A metallic tinge of blood coats the air. It smells god awful and reminds me of death. It's been quiet for days since we've been back and there's no reason to fear an attack, but that fucking smell makes my skin crawl and my body shake with anxiousness. The scent gets stronger and I find myself picking up my pace as a sick churning stirs in my stomach. *My mate.*

I grip the doorknob so tightly it nearly breaks off in my grasp as the door bashes violently against the wall. Veronica's form is a blur as she spins to face me. Seeing she's safe calms the beast clawing inside me. My frantic breathing eases as I walk to her. The sense of peace is fleeting as I study her face.

With wide eyes so black they match the silk negligee she wears, my mate looks as though she's been caught with her hand in the cookie jar. I grin and look past her to the large walnut desk. My smile falls instantly. My mate swallows and opens her mouth, but I silence her with a glare.

At least a dozen blood bags line its polished surface. They've been opened and drained, and it looks like she's been scraping the insides of the bag with a razor. There's a small pile of white powder in the center of the desk. The poison. She's collecting the poison designed to corrupt her immortality.

Unable to breathe, I stare into her eyes and search for an answer.

This isn't real. It can't be true. Disbelief comes in waves. What the hell is she doing with this shit? My blood runs cold as all manner of possibilities race through me.

"Did you drink the blood?" That's the first concern on my mind. I don't think my mate would hurt herself by drinking this shit. She can't. She wouldn't.

She drinks from me daily. I can give her everything she needs.

"No." Her voice is small and her eyes are brimming with bloodied tears.

I nod my head and back away from the desk, walking to the bed with my back to her. If she's collecting this drug, it can't be for anything good. I think of any enemy she could have that's vampire, but I come up with nothing. I haven't the faintest clue why she would be harvesting this weapon. And it's one fucked-up weapon. They found four vampires at the warehouse; their fangs were barely visible and their immortality gone. Two were already dead and the other two were no stronger than humans. They needed a complete blood transfusion and to be bitten and turned again. They're still weak, though, nowhere near the vampires they used to be. There's no reason Veronica should have this shit here.

What the fuck is she doing? Did her queen give her orders without me knowing?

"Explain." The single word falls hard between us. I hope she can sense my disappointment and the agony at being kept in the dark. She's up to something, something of grave proportions. If she's hurting and planning revenge, she should've told me. Why wouldn't my own mate confide in me?

"I don't want this anymore." Her chest rises and falls with the admission, pain laced in her tone.

What the fuck? My heart sinks at her words. A spiked lump forms in my throat. She doesn't want me anymore? If she thinks she can run from me, she's dead fucking wrong. I'll always find her and bring her back to me.

"What have I done that makes you want to leave me?" Her head tilts and confusion is easily read on her face.

A beat passes and a hard lump grows in my throat.

"Why would I want to leave you?" Her softly spoken question instantly eases my body and I struggle to hide the fact that I'm fucking crumbling on the inside.

"You said you don't want this anymore?" I need her to clarify her words, and I fucking hope it's something I can handle. Because this shit is fucked beyond recognition and I'm failing to see what the hell is going on.

"I—" Her eyes look around the room as if searching for an answer I'll find acceptable.

I move into her space and growl out the words, "Answer me."

She stares straight into my eyes as she speaks, "I don't want to be immortal. I can't live when you die. I don't want to. I don't want this. A life without you isn't one worth living."

I stare into her dark eyes as my heart clenches in agony. My poor mate. Taking her head in my hands, I kiss her plump lips and lick across the seam for her to part for me. My tongue rubs along her bottom lip and caresses hers, while I allow the pain to subside and find the words to give her peace.

What do I know of immortality and how she's feeling? I know I would want to die if she was taken from me. I wouldn't want to go on without her. But my mate is strong and is destined to live once I've been buried in the dirt. I would never wish her to be in pain, but to want her to give up her immortality? Never.

I part from her and miss the warmth immediately. "What about our children? You're blessed to be able to care for them and watch them grow once I'm gone. You'll have peace loving them when I can't."

Tears fall from her eyes. "I don't know that I can ever give you pups, Vince." She sniffs and turns her back to me to take a tissue from the package on the desk. How did I not know this? How have I let myself be so blind to the cost of her immortality.

"You think this poison will give you that ability?"

"I don't know, but it's worth it to try if it can."

My head spins. How could she be so reckless? "But we haven't even tried without resorting to something like this. Something that could destroy you!"

She lifts her chin and defiantly tells me, "I will give it all up to be the mate you deserve!"

"You are the mate I deserve, Veronica. You're more than that." I push her against the wall and cage her in with my body. She moves easily, not resisting in the least. "Tell me you haven't taken the drug. Please tell me you haven't."

Her shoulders shake with her sobs and then she says, "Only a little." I feel my heart fall and the crushing weight of guilt push through my limbs.

"Veronica." I place a hand on her neck and kiss my mark on the other side. "Don't. Don't do this. I love you just the way you are. I don't want this. I just want you."

"But I want to give you more. I want to be more for you." My head shakes at her words.

"How can you think so little of yourself? You're

perfect in every way." I kiss her forehead as tears slip down my cheeks. "I've failed you as a mate." Her hands shove against my chest.

"Don't you dare say that; you've shown me glimpses of the kind of life that is possible without the burden of immortality. You've given me hope and desire for more. How could you think you've failed me?"

"You're drugging yourself to be something you're not!" She cowers from my words and the sinking feeling of defeat races through me. "Promise me you won't take any more." She refuses to look at me and sobs harder. "Promise me, Veronica." She slowly shakes her head, but I'm not going to accept that. There has to be another way.

"Just wait for me, then." Her eyes finally find mine at my desperate words. "We can try without it. We can wait until the Authority is done with their testing." I pull her into my arms and let her head rest against my shoulder. I stroke her back and settle some as her breathing relaxes. "We can try without it." I kiss her hair, inhaling the sweet floral scent of jasmine and add, "We have time to wait."

"I'll wait." She whispers the words.

"Promise me. Promise me you'll tell me if you think about it again."

"I will, I promise."

I kiss her hair again. "We can try without it. I will give you everything you need. I promise you, my love." She sniffles and kisses the crook of my neck. The feel of her soft lips against my skin brings a warmth to my chilled blood. "I love you, Veronica."

"I will love you forever, Vince."

ABOUT THE AUTHOR

Thank you so much for reading my romances. I'm just a stay at home mom and avid reader turned author and I couldn't be happier.

I hope you love my books as much as I do!

More by Willow Winters
www.WillowWintersWrites.com/books

9 798888 592781 9